A PLANET CALLED HEAVEN

Borgo Press Books by Ardath Mayhar

The Absolutely Perfect Horse: A Young Adult Novel (with Marylois Dunn)
The Body in the Swamp: An Occult Mystery
Carrots and Miggle: A Novel of East Texas
The Clarrington Heritage
Closely Knit in Scarlatt
Crazy Quilt: The Best Short Stories of Ardath Mayhar
Deadly Memoir
Death in the Square
The Door in the Hill: A Tale of the Turnipins
The Dropouts: A Tale of Growing Up in East Texas
Feud at Sweetwater Creek: A Novel of the Old West
The Fugitives: A Tale of Prehistoric Times
The Heirs of Three Oaks: A Novel of the Old West
High Mountain Winter: A Novel of the Old West
How the Gods Wove in Kyrannon: Tales of the Triple Moons
Hunters of the Plains: A Novel of Prehistoric America
Island in the Lake: A Novel of Native America
Khi to Freedom: A Science Fiction Novel
The Lintons of Skillet Bend: A Novel of East Texas
Lone Runner: A Novel of the Old West
Lords of the Triple Moons: Tales of the Triple Moons
Makra Choria: A Novel of High Fantasy
Medicine Dream: Being the Further Adventures of Burr Henderson
Messengers in White: A Science Fantasy Novel
Monkey Station: A Novel of the Future (Macaque Cycle #1; with Ron Fortier)
People of the Mesa: A Novel of Native America
A Planet Called Heaven: A Science Fiction Novel
Prescription for Danger: A Novel of the Old West
Reflections; & Journey to an Ending: Collected Poems
A Road of Stars: A Fantasy of Life, Death, Love, and Art
Runes of the Lyre: A Science Fantasy Novel
The Saga of Grittel Sundotha: A Science Fantasy Novel
The Seekers of Shar-Nuhn: Tales of the Triple Moons
Shock Treatment: An Account of Granary's War
Slewfoot Sally and the Flying Mule: Tall Tales from Cotton County, Texas
Soul-Singer of Tyrnos: A Fantasy Novel
Strange Doings in the Pine Hills: Stories
Through a Stone Wall: Lessons from Thirty Years of Writing
Timber Pirates: A Novel of East Texas (with Marylois Dunn)
Towers of the Earth: A Novel of Native America
Trail of the Seahawks: A Novel of the Future (Macaque Cycle #2; with R. Fortier)
The Tulpa: A Novel of Fantasy
Two-Moons and the Black Tower: A Novel of Fantasy
Vendetta
Warlock's Gift: Tales of the Triple Moons
The World Ends in Hickory Hollow: A Novel of the Future
A World of Weirdities: Tales to Shiver By

A PLANET CALLED HEAVEN

A Science Fiction Novel

by

Ardath Mayhar

THE BORGO PRESS

An Imprint of Wildside Press LLC

MMIX

CONTENTS

A PLANET CALLED HEAVEN

FOREWORD

The world from which the Family Thomas is sent is not a pretty one, but in many ways it is little worse than that in which all too many families live in this world to-day. A fresh beginning is always frightening, but I understand those who can cope with change and danger. My own family did something similar when I was a child, and then my husband and I took a blind leap of faith when our sons were still small.

Being afraid is not cowardice but good sense, in some circumstances. Letting fear prevent you from doing what is necessary—that is cowardice.

—Ardath Mayhar
Chireno, Texas
October 2007

ABOUT THE AUTHOR

The author of sixty-two books, more than forty of them published commercially, **Ardath Mayhar** began her career in the early eighties with science fiction novels from Doubleday and TSR. Atheneum published several of her young adult and children's novels. Changing focus, she wrote westerns (as **Frank Cannon**) and mountain man novels (as **John Killdeer**), four prehistoric Indian books under her own name, and historical western *High Mountain Winter* under the byline **Frances Hurst**.

Recently she has been working with on-line publishers. *A Road of Stars* was her first original novel to appear in print-on-demand format. Many of her out-of-print titles are now available from e-publishers fictionwise.com and renebooks.com; many other novels are being published by the Borgo Press Imprint of Wildside Press and Amazon.com.

Now in her seventies, Mayhar was widowed in 1999, after forty-one years of marriage, and has four grown sons. She now works at home, writing short fiction and nonfiction, and doing book doctoring professionally. Her web pages can be found at:

w2.netdot.com/ardathm/ and
http://ofearna.us/ books/mayhar.html

PART ONE

THE SPACE FAMILY THOMAS

A Planet Called Heaven, by Ardath Mayhar

CHAPTER ONE

But Where Will We Go?

No matter how crowded and dirty the city became, the Thomas home was always a place where people began to smile when they came in at the door. Not that it was a fancy place—it certainly was not. The Thomases had no more or less than any other poor family who lived in the Block, but what they did with what they had was very different.

The hallways on either side of their entry were scrawled with names and messages and words as dirty as the paint, but on either side of their own door the plaster was scrubbed to an even gray. The street beyond the outer set of grillwork barriers was awash with the unwashed, as Mama often said, though her own children were kept clean. The gutters were filled with empty bottles and cans and passed-out Dopies and even, sometimes, dead ones.

Anthea, hurrying back from an errand to the food depot or the clothes-wash place, always began to hum as she unlocked the grill with her handprint, scurried up the long-stalled escalator, and found herself at the door of her own apartment. Beyond the wood and metal barrier were order and warmth, a clean, safe haven amid the dangers of the city.

Coming home now with her arms burdened with bundles of clean wash and their food ration for the week, Anthea found herself wondering why others in the Block did not make their own homes clean and pleasant, too. This vast government-run tenement was supposed to provide safety and shelter for those who lived here. Instead it seemed to breed troublemakers like rats. Even more like rats, they seemed to like their own filth.

She found her sister, Hannah, on her knees in the hall, scrubbing away at the worn plastic floor covering. Someone had bled there, in the night, and dried blood was hard to remove. Still, their corridor never smelled the way those others in the Block did, and their home was free of the stench of dirty people and old food.

Mama heard her coming and opened the door, saving her the trouble of ringing the bell. The smell of soap and soup wafted into the hall as Anthea stepped into the apartment and began handing out clean laundry to her family. The wash-up place provided free machines, free soap, and there was no excuse for being dirty, as Mama so often reminded them.

Their neighbors thought they were crazy, of course, but that was all right. They were Thomases, and that was enough.

As she handed the last batch of underwear and clean shirts to Van, the oldest of them all, she realized he looked...strange. She had been so busy with her task she didn't notice, at first, the unusual silence in the room.

She turned to look at Mama. Tears were standing in her dark eyes, just ready to spill over.

Anthea felt a jolt of fear. She had not seen Mama cry since Father died, four years ago when she was ten. Who...? She counted frantically, but there were still seven people in the room. With herself and Hannah, out in the hallway, it came to five Thomases and four cousins. What had happened while she was gone?

"Mama?" Her voice squeaked, and she cleared her throat.

"We got this. Just now the man came around to all the people in the Block and gave us these. Oh, Anthea! Oh, Anthea! It is so hard to keep things going, and then to have something like this...." Mama turned away and wiped her eyes on the back of her brown hand.

Anthea looked down, dreading what might be written on the paper she held.

NOTICE TO ALL
NON-CONTRIBUTING PERSONNEL

it said. She caught her breath. Non-contributing, indeed! She worked four days a week at the child-care center, and all her family held what jobs they could find, as often as they were available. Mama, more than any of them, worked hard at keeping things clean, making the tasteless rations from the center into something palatable, and nursing sick neighbors, no matter how slack-twisted they might be.

She shook her head and looked again at the paper:

All nonessential personnel are to be relocated, as quickly as may be done, to colony worlds. These have been carefully prepared for your arrival and are in every way suitable for human existence. The inhabitants of City 136 have been assigned to Heaven, a planet well capable of sustaining life, suitable for survival and promising eventual prosperity.

The Council of Overlords has decreed the cities are to be evacuated in order of their numbers, and City 136 will be emptied of its people within one hundred and twenty days of your receipt of this order. Personal possessions will be limited to five pounds per individual, none of which can be books or other illegal materials.

Equipment and clothing will be provided on-planet for your use. It has been decided this will be held to a minimum, however, in order to motivate new colonists to learn to live in and with their new homes as quickly as possible.

HOLDOUTS WILL SUFFER THE FULL PENALTY OF THE LAW

Anthea shivered. Her father had defied the law, years before, and she knew what the penalty would be. In a system of worlds so crowded with unneeded people, death was dealt out easily and often. Her father had died for a book! The precious volume had been taken away with him, and she was certain it had been destroyed, though she still recalled, almost word-for-word, the stories she had heard him read aloud from its pages, when she was tiny.

The Elephant's Child. That was one of them. *How the Rhinoceros Got His Skin.* Wonderful stories had lived inside its covers, filled with words that sang!

She felt a tug at her elbow. Mama held out her arms, and Anthea laid her head on the familiar shoulder and let her tears soak Mama's regulation gray shirt.

"We are Thomases," came a whisper in her ear. "We will survive, and we will not allow the Council of Overlords or anyone else to make us forget that!"

Over Mama's shoulder, she could see Van cuddling Sarah, the baby. She was five, usually too grown up for such things, but now she was burrowing into his shoulder as if to hide from this suddenly hostile world. The four little cousins, Mark, David, Elton, and Sty, were huddled together, their small shoulders hunched as if waiting for another blow, even worse than the one that left them parentless.

Anthea straightened and wiped her eyes. "You're right," she said to her mother. She knelt and put her arms around her small cousins. "We're Thomases, no matter what happens."

But at the bottom of her heart she felt a cold nudge of fear. Not one of them had ever had any training that would help them survive on a strange world. The City was all they knew, for the farmlands were rigorously fenced away from the city folk, and walls rose to shield them from the wistful gazes of those lucky enough to live near them.

How could a people whose feet had never touched real soil, whose eyes had never seen a tree or a shrub or even healthy grass, learn to grow their own food? What would allow them to make their unaided way on a world where there would never be any help at all?

Anthea, even though she was only fourteen, understood with sudden clear insight that the Council had no intention of checking on those "colony worlds" again. They were vast scrap-heaps, where all these billions of unwanted people were to be dumped, scattered over incredible reaches of space, along the remote arms of the galaxy that would never be visited.

CHAPTER TWO

Upheaval

Although the Thomases had very little in the way of clothing and furniture and personal items, that made the things they did have even more precious. Anthea treasured a chunk of bright stone Van had found in the garbage once, and brought home to her. It was streaked with swirls of greeny-cream and dark red-brown, and it was the only beautiful thing in the apartment.

It, alone, weighed almost the allotted five pounds, and she knew it would have to stay behind. Her clean underwear and the note her father had given her when he knew he would be taken away were all she could pack for the journey that lay before them.

Mama sorted and worried and counted necessary things like toothbrushes and soap, but there was no way to take enough clean things to keep the family decent on a long voyage. It was with actual relief that Anthea found a fresh directive in their mail slot. This one was brief and to the point:

TRANSIT WILL TAKE PLACE
IN CRYOGENIC SUSPENSION

CLOTHING AND OTHER NECESSITIES
WILL BE PROVIDED AT YOUR
DESTINATION

DO NOT PACK SUCH ITEMS

Mama almost smiled when she handed it to her. "We will sleep all the way! This means we can take some things that really mean something," she sighed. "Like your father's photograph. And grandmother's handmade lace shawl."

"Sarah's doll?" asked Hannah, popping up from behind the couch, where she had been trying to fit her own things into a small packet. "What about Lutetia?"

Anthea and her mother stared at each other. Lutetia was almost one of the family. Made by Mama, with an embroidered face and synthasilk hair, she was the size of a three-year-old and must weigh at least five or six pounds. And Sarah would be completely shattered if her doll had to be left behind—she had had it all her life, and it was as much her sister as Anthea or Hannah.

Mama frowned, her eyebrows almost meeting over her nose. Then her eyes brightened. "I know. Hannah, get my scissors. We'll take the stuffing out. Then, when we get there, we will find something, if it is only dried grass, and stuff her full again. Empty, she won't weigh anything much."

Hannah scrambled for the scissors in a shackledy drawer, while Anthea pulled the doll's dress off and exposed her seams.

"Hurry, before Sarah and Van come back. She won't understand. We can tell her we have already packed Lutetia," Mama said, sitting in the ancient rocking chair to disembowel the toy.

She just made it. As Anthea folded the empty "skin" of Lutetia, along with the dress and underwear, into the package of items for Sarah, the child burst into the room, full of excitement.

"Everybody is going away!" she shouted, whirling round and round on her chubby heels. "Everybody is leaving and going up into the sky-y-y!"

Van, behind her, tried to smile, but he knew too well what this great moving day meant. "The Transits are outside, and everybody on the first floor is already out. We'll be next—this afternoon, the officer said. Is everything ready?"

"We just settled the last item." His mother nodded toward Sarah. "We found a way to pack up Lutetia with the rest of our treasures. Do you have your packet ready?"

"With the others," said Van. He sighed and reached for the child's whirling hand. "Stop now, Sarah. This afternoon, we'll go too. So let's go and say goodbye to the tree."

Nothing else could have calmed the child so quickly. There was only one tree in the lives of anyone in City 136, and that was the straggly oak some blocks away, which was the only survivor of what had once been a large and beautiful park.

When the Overlords had taken over the government of Terra, they had objected to the waste of land space and ordered all the trees cut down. The oak had been saved because it grew between the walk and the street, and through all the years since it had held on, gritty with dust and soot, half strangled with fumes from the factories.

Still, it was green in summer, and a bird nested in it almost every spring. It was the TREE—the only one the people in the Blocks had ever seen, and leaving it was going to be a wrench for many of the children.

Van carried Sarah away, and her small face was sober with the sudden realization of just what this migration was going to mean to her and her kin. When the door closed behind them and the locks were shot, Mama gathered all the small packets together on the table beside the door and made certain each was labeled with the name of its owner.

The small boys' things were skimpy, even for such a limited allowance. They had come away from City 837, after the Transit accident that killed their parents, with only the clothing on their backs, the heirloom watch their father had thrust into David's hand at the last moment before getting onto the Transit with their mother, and a burden of fear and uncertainty in their hearts. Even a year of being part of her aunt's family had not completely reassured them, and this move was doing nothing to help.

Anthea, at a glance from her mother, went into the bedroom shared by all the boys. The small brothers were huddled together on the big bed, their faces scarlet with suppressed tears. Their hands (a bit grubby about the knuckles, Anthea noted from old habit) were locked together as if they could never part again.

She perched on the edge of the bed. "Listen, fellows," she said. "We're all going together. And Mama has done something wonderful. We're all going to be Thomases.

"She listed you as her children, the last time the census man came, and nobody cared enough to investigate. So you will go with us, for they aren't going to split up families. This is the one thing they say that I believe."

Mark, who was nine, straightened up and wiped his eyes on his gray sleeve. "We're Thomases?" His voice shook, but he seemed cheered by the thought. "Not Nortons, any more?"

"You'll always be Nortons when you think of your Daddy and your Mom, but you're Thomases from now on as far as anybody outside the family is concerned," she said, her tone firmer than she actually felt.

"Now come on, boys. It will be time to go before you know it. You need to get cleaned up for one last time. We're going to sleep all the way to Heaven! Can you believe that?"

They straggled into the inadequate bathroom, one by one, to shower and change into their best and cleanest clothing. "Wear your good shoes!" she called.

Who knew when they would get more? And their feet grew almost from day to day. She sighed and rose. "Come when you're ready," she called, closing the door behind her. *Ready or not!* she thought suddenly.

The afternoon came more quickly than she liked. When the Transits pulled up before the main entry to the Block, a shout went up from the officers in charge of the evacuation. "Second floor out!"

A hum of activity rose at once, as people streamed from their apartments, carrying their skimpy packets of possessions. Mama, her brood ranked behind her with Van and Anthea at the end to prevent straggling, waited until the officer with the census roll came to her door to check off the tenants of her rooms.

"Thomas," said the broad-shouldered woman, whose black eyes surveyed the group as if they were furniture to be counted. "Caroline, thirty-nine, parent; Van, sixteen, oldest male offspring; Anthea, fourteen, oldest female; Hannah, twelve; Mark, nine; David, eight; Elton, six; Sarah, five; Stuyvesant, four."

She stared at Mama. "People like you are the reason the worlds are too crowded. You ought to be ashamed. You deserve to be sent off to...." She caught herself and shut her mouth.

Mama didn't even look at her as she led her family down the corridor. She never worried about the opinions of people who didn't know what they were talking about.

Anthea glanced curiously into open doors along the hall. Never was a door left open, ordinarily, and she had only caught brief glimpses of those other apartments as neighbors went in or came out of them. Now they stood wide open to view, their furniture just like that in her own, though more battered and dingy-looking. She suspected none of the wood had seen polish in generations.

The hall was full of jostling groups, old and young, families and singles. Even those whom Caroline had nursed through sickness or injury didn't seem to see her, as they stumbled toward the waiting Transit.

On each face Anthea could see the reflection of the fear and uncertainty she felt, but she hoped she was concealing hers better. The children would be frightened, if she showed what she was actually feeling.

As she reached the wide doors, she turned to look back. The corridor was still full of people, but she could see drifts of dropped bundles, confiscated possessions the officers had taken from those who were leaving, and garbage that had not yet been collected for the week.

She turned back to follow the children into the long tube of the Transit. No matter where they were sent, what was or was not there, she suspected it had to be better than City 136.

As the Transit filled, the air grew stale with unwashed bodies and overcrowding. Sarah, in Mama's lap, suddenly burst into tears, but her voice couldn't be heard over the wails and shrieks of other people's children, who already had realized their world was about to change drastically and forever.

Van held Sty on his lap and had his arms about Elton and David. Mark was huddled against Anthea, and Hannah, on her other side, was trembling silently. Now the time had come, there was no way to guess what would happen next. A spaceship? They had never seen even a picture of one.

Cryogenic sleep? It sounded too much like dying to be a comfortable thought. Anthea, too, shivered until she caught Mama's eye. Then she straightened her back, hugged Hannah and Mark to her sides, and kept the stiff upper lip that was the hallmark of a Thomas.

The port was hours away from City 136. Night covered the countryside, which seemed, from what Anthea could see before twilight leached away, to be row upon row of housing complexes. Some looked to be homes of the wealthy, for trees grew around them and bright flower boxes lined the windows. Others were as grim and ugly as the Blocks.

Just before it was too dark to see, they passed a long stretch of farmland. Green stretches spread into the distance, beyond the wall, and the rise of the land allowed those riding high in the Transit to see out over the acres of plants.

Corn? Anthea wondered. She had heard the word, but she had no way of knowing if the rustling rows of plants might be that or something else. She sank back into her seat, as they drew away from the farmland, and thought about how she and her family could survive on a world whose plants might be poisonous to them.

No promise made by the Overlords was ever kept, much less believed by those who lived under their callous rule. Anthea wondered if this journey was a sentence of death, but then she realized there were far easier and less expensive ways to dispose of excess people. A thousand years in the past, according to her history lessons, an Earthling ruler had used such methods, and his name was still spoken with a shudder.

No, if people were being sent off in spaceships, it must be in order to try claiming distant worlds for the System by planting colonists on them. That made a kind of sense, even if the Overlords might never need or want those worlds again. They had a habit of taking more than they could use and then neglecting it.

The Transits slowed, the line of tubes turning into a broad avenue leading into the spaceport. Clusters of lights, yellow and red and green, winked on and off, marking off embarkation areas. The Transits followed them and pulled into a row alongside a tremendous building, into which all their passengers were herded.

Now it was hard to keep the family together, and Mama linked them together, hand to hand, with the smallest ones carried by Van and herself. "We are all we have," she murmured into their ears as she put them into position. "We mustn't lose anybody."

Inside the building, the families were shunted into smaller chambers, each of which held a line of people in white coats. They whisked through the lists of evacuees briskly, a family at a time, checking each member off on a master roll.

At the end was a screened area, and as they approached, a nurse made sure sleeves would not get into the way. "Preliminary shots," she said, again and again, in a weary tone.

When the time came, Anthea did not flinch. Neither did even the smallest Thomases, who were now almost in shock at the sudden upheaval in their lives.

At once, they were laid on rolling cots, still together in a line, and as they were pushed toward a long corridor, Anthea felt her eyes growing heavy. The shot was putting her to sleep.

She struggled to hold her eyelids open. "Mama?" she moaned.

"Hush!" came a sharp voice into her ear. "You will be together. You may not like your destination, but you will arrive together. Now sleep!"

The voice was hurried, but its tone was so sure she relaxed and let herself drift, hearing the swish of cot-wheels and the distant drone of something—engines?

As she sank into a black well of sleep, she wondered if she had heard the engines of the shuttle that would take her family up to the waiting ship.

CHAPTER THREE

New Worries on a New World

Something was bothering Van. He tried to shake away the intruding element and sink again into the long sleep, but his own body was determined to wake, and there was nothing he could do to stop it. Vitality tickled along his veins, and Van's groggy mind finally remembered.

They had arrived. The drugs to wake him from his cryogenic sleep had been administered, and it was time to go out into a world he couldn't even imagine and help his family to survive there. That thought did more than the drugs to make him pull his mind and body out of the mists of sleep.

The family! Were they all alive and well? The Overlords had assured everyone the long sleep was perfectly safe, but he had heard talk, read illegal newssheets, and he knew a certain percentage of those undergoing the Cold Transit did not wake at the other end of their journey.

He rose from the bin in which he had crossed space, pushing himself to overcome the remnants of the treatment. He had to find the others and make certain all was well.

Others in the layered bins were not waking as quickly as he. He climbed down the ladder, past groans and grunts of awakening people, to stand at last on the gray floor and stare about, reading the lists posted at the end of each tier of Cold Sleep bins.

That reassured him a bit—families did, indeed, seem to have been kept together. Thomases of all kinds were in the tier from which he had just climbed.

He peered at the list, having trouble focusing his eyes. Amos, Andrew, Anna, Anthea! He ran his finger down to the C's. And there was Caroline. The boys and Hannah and Sarah were all here, near him. He turned as a step rasped on the plastic flooring behind him.

"Well, you are a quick one, aren't you?" The young woman held a clipboard and a vial of something that she turned and injected into the system of tubing linking all the bins. "You won't even need the booster to get you going. Most do."

She seemed normal and friendly, and he ventured to ask, "How long will it be? I have family still asleep here." He felt himself shiver, his briefs leaving most of his skin bare.

She turned to a cubicle set into the wall and handed him a poncho-like robe. "Here. Put this on. Your circulation isn't going well, yet, and you're going to be cold anyway, for this is not a very warm world. Go down to the end of this chamber and turn right. There will be hot soup there. That should make you feel better."

He obeyed her instructions, even though he would have liked to stay and talk with her. She wasn't more than twenty, and she was prettier than any girl he had ever seen in the Blocks. Her hair was shiny brown, neatly braided, and her skin glowed with cleanliness and health. But she was busy, and he knew it was time to catch up with himself, before he had the others to think about.

The long room into which he went was lined with tables and benches, all fastened to the floor. As soon as he entered the room, the computer voice said, "One soup. One wake-up tea. Sit in section number thirty, place nine."

He took the gray tray from the slot below the speaker and walked carefully, so as not to splash either soup or tea on the robe he wore. The liquids were very hot, and as he sipped the tea, he found his body responded more easily, his mind cleared even more from the mists of the drugs. His stomach, so long unused to food, woke, too, and began to growl.

He had spooned up several mouthfuls of broth before the next sleeper arrived. That one, to his relief, was Hannah. She saw him and moved to sit by him, ignoring the orders of the computer. She looked a bit pale, and blue circles ringed her brown eyes, but as she sipped her own tea she began to look better.

"We're here," said Van, suddenly ill at ease with her, in this strange place. "Did you see Mama or Anthea or any of the little ones?"

"Mama's waking up. They have just about everybody moving. But, Van, I think there's something wrong with Sty. They wouldn't let Mama look at him, and the lady seemed worried. Do you suppose...do you think he's all right?"

"The Overlords swore this was as safe as taking the Transit. Safer." His own words did nothing to reassure him, for everyone knew the Overlords said whatever would serve their purposes best. Truth was not a thing he expected from them.

Even as he spoke, he remembered his earlier thoughts on the subject. Was Sty going to be one of those unlucky ones who didn't make it through? He shivered and reached to cuddle his sister to his side. Their ponchos rustled together, as they clung for a moment before returning to the food.

When Mama came, it was with Sarah in her arms. She, too, ignored the directions of the computer, after getting her tray, and sat with Van and Hannah. "What can they do to us now?" she asked, when the computer rattled off a string of instructions. "Deport me?" There was no laughter in her voice.

Not being programmed to reply to sarcasm, the speaker went silent, and Mama slid into place on the other side of Hannah and began sipping her tea while watching to make sure Sarah didn't spill any of hers. "I suspect there won't be any seconds," she said. "So you be careful. Drink it all and eat all of that soup. You need it."

Van looked at her over Hannah's head, hoping she would understand the question in his eyes.

She shook her head. "We don't know yet. Anthea and Mark were sick when they woke up, but there is medication to settle that and it is fairly normal. Elton is taking his time, but he will be all right. David is having a tantrum, and I wasn't up to coping with it, though the young woman in charge seems to be able to handle almost anything.

"But Sty—they closed his bin, after she checked on him. I think—Van, I'm dreadfully afraid he didn't make it." Her eyes filled with tears, but she took a hasty sip of tea to cover them.

Van reached around Hannah and patted his mother's shoulder. "He might...he might be luckier than we are, Mama. If he didn't make it, he won't have to face whatever it is that's out there, below the ship's orbit." And suddenly he believed his own words.

The long room was filling, now, with people in gray ponchos, and as they approached the table at which the Thomases sat, a quiet request from Mama saved places for the rest of her brood.

At last, Anthea came through the door, her face as gray as her poncho, with Mark holding onto her, as much to support her weight as to comfort himself. Elton and David, the latter's face stained with recent tears, held onto her poncho as they threaded their way among the long tables to reach the spot where Mama was waving frantically to get their attention.

The young woman in the white coat came after them, her own face pinched and pale. She bent over the end of the table as she spoke to Mama. "I am so sorry, Mrs. Thomas. The least boy—he simply didn't respond normally to the drugs and the cold. He—won't be waking up." She looked as if she might cry, too.

Mama took her hand and squeezed it. "I knew it, I think, from the time I woke enough to understand what was going on. But don't cry. I don't blame you. I blame the Overlords."

The girl looked both shocked and frightened. "Oh, please! Don't talk like that!"

Mama stared up into her eyes. "We have been sent to a place we didn't want to go. We are about to be abandoned here, along with thousands of other people who don't want to be here, either.

"If they killed us at this moment, we might be better off, so I shall say what I think. But I won't get you into trouble. You go back to work, and don't think about little Sty. I would like to believe that, wherever he is, he is with his parents, whatever the New Priesthood tries to tell us."

The girl turned to go. Then she looked back. "I am Janna. Janna Hobart. Remember—I did try to help!" And then she hurried back to her duties, leaving the Thomases staring at each other, their faces grim.

"She did, you know," said Caroline. "She did her best for every one of us. And most of the others have, too, if you think about it. It isn't the people carrying out the orders whom we can blame. They're caught in the same trap we are in.

"The Overlords—they are the ones to blame. As far as I know, not one of them has ever visited Terra or even seen an Earthman who wasn't some sort of flunkey or diplomat. They don't care."

Her eyes kindled sparks. "Children, listen to me. We never would have had a chance on a world run by such a system. Here, it can be different. There are no Overlords here, whatever anyone may say. This is a world we can handle in our own way. So don't be afraid. No matter what is down there, it has to be better than what we left behind."

Van felt his heart ease, the cold lump that had formed there seeming to melt in the fire of her words. This was a new world. He was young and fairly strong and ready to tackle anything.

Suddenly he felt excitement ripple through his nerves. He looked up to find Anthea staring at him, her pale face beginning to take on color. She, too, had caught the implications of their mother's words.

This was a world they could shape to suit themselves, if that was possible at all. And if the world did not cooperate, then they could shape themselves to suit it, instead of being rammed, protesting, into the mold designed by those who controlled the System that ran all the worlds they knew.

CHAPTER FOUR

An Alien World

The shuttle took the passengers down a hundred at a time. Even then, it required days to transfer all of the thousands from City 136 to their new home, and days more were occupied in planeting and setting up the Shelter Dome, which was to provide housing and food and warmth for them until they could learn to make their own.

Van watched through the viewplate as the shuttle carrying the Thomases spun through thin wisps of cloud toward the huge gray-brown ball below. He could see a thin rim of ocean shining at one edge, as well as shadow-wrinkled areas that seemed to be deep canyons. He could clearly see a huge polar ice-cap.

Glints of streams were visible, but very far apart. This was not a wet world, it was plain, but one whose water was mostly locked up in ice, if that ice-cap meant anything. Almost a quarter of the planet was covered with it, and he knew the other pole would be similar. That meant winters would probably be very harsh.

The shuttle leveled, and Janna ordered everyone into harness for the landing. When the shuttle had upended itself and the stomach-wrenching landing was done, the doors slipped aside to allow the people to slide down the chutes.

Van peered through the remnants of the dust left by their descent and saw a colorless landscape spreading away to a horizon that seemed unbelievably distant to someone reared amid the canyons of a city. He could walk for days, without reaching anything within view, he was sure.

Caroline and Anthea had the family in line again, each child gripping his or her small packet of personal items. As they came to rest at the bottom of the chute, the older members of the family gathered them again into order and followed Janna toward a temporary tent-shelter. Van straggled behind, looking around him with unbelieving eyes.

The sky clamped down over the land in a tremendous dome, smoothly at the edge of the flat lands to the north, with uneven ups and downs to the south and west. The setting sun had turned the dusty plain to orange, and the shuttle itself was flaming gold.

The air seemed a bit thin, but it was clean! Never in all his sixteen years had Van smelled air that was uncontaminated by human waste and garbage. This was almost intoxicating, and he breathed so deeply it almost made him dizzy.

There were scents borne on the wind, but they were so alien he could not name one. It was almost a relief to get into the familiar stinks of the tent, where the others from the shuttle were being issued clothing and equipment.

"This is a relatively unknown world," a tall young man was saying, as he passed items to Janna, who handed them to those waiting in line. "There may be predators that did not show up on the preliminary scans. We are issuing LCF staffs to all colonists over the age of twelve."

Janna bent to listen as someone whispered into her ear. When she straightened again, she said, "For those of you who wonder, LCF stands for Limited Controlled Fusion. These staffs use a non-radioactive substance called lithium, which can create heat energy without dangerous emissions.

"The principal sources of energy in your Dome will be LCF units. The staffs can be used as weapons or as tools, according to the manner in which you adjust the beams, and they will last for many generations without any except solar charging. By that time, your descendants should not need them any longer, having adapted to the ways of this particular world."

The young man had waited impatiently as the girl explained. Now he began handing out staffs and bundles again. "In these packages are clothing, items for personal hygiene, even small games and instruction manuals with diagrams for dealing with wood-working, planting, and animals that may be tamed for domestic use.

"There are supplies that will be stored in your Dome, to replace those worn out, broken, or otherwise made unusable, but these are limited and we urge that you learn as soon as possible to work with the things available on this world."

Van inched along until he had his own staff in one hand, his bundle in the other. Ahead of him, Caroline shepherded the younger children out of the tent and into a broad area filled with busy people. The Dome was going up, and everyone who expected to live in it was also expected to help raise it.

They put their things together, set Sarah to care for them, and looked about for things they could do to help. A burly man seemed to have taken charge, though he was certainly not one of the officers or crew of the ship.

"You, there, young people! Help those men carry sections over to the far wall. Ma'am, you and the little ones can sit here and sort bolts. Made sure the nuts fit onto the bolts they're matched with. When you get a pile done, the young ones can put them in this bucket and carry them over there."

He pointed to the spot at which a team of people were fitting together the big thermoplast segments, which were being formed from the soil of the plain by a large machine, and fastening them with three sizes of bolts.

"Why in thunder they didn't make them all the same size I couldn't tell you. Makes a lot more work. But what else can you expect of Them?" He turned away to bellow an order and seemed to forget about the Thomases.

The shuttle went back and forth to the ship, and those on the ground went forward with assembling their temporary home. Van donned his new clothing, which, though gray, as was everything designed by the Overlords, was stout and promised to wear well.

He and Anthea were glad of the hard work, for the wind skimming the plain was chilly, except at mid-day.

His mother and the others had to wear their poncho cloaks, as they sat sorting bolts.

* * * * * * *

Days passed, and long nights in which groups of exiles sat around big fires built of the scrubby brush covering the plain. Sleeping bags were passed out every evening, made of thin stuff that allowed every grain of sand to make its own individual imprint in the skin of the sleeper, but they were warm and even kept their tenants dry, when a sudden storm blew up, with gusting wind and intermittent rain.

In seventeen days, the Dome was completed. The LCF unit was brought down from the ship and installed in the shelter, and this unusual heating system was put into operation. Now the nights were spent inside, out of the cold wind, and the presence of ten thousand human bodies triggered the system to work at maximum capacity.

Van found himself comfortable for the first time in what seemed years, and his only regret was that the ship would leave soon. He had come to know Janna well, and some of the other crew members, too. He felt they were friends, and he knew he would never see them again, once the shuttle carried them off-planet.

The morning arrived for their departure, and everyone was up and outside long before the shuttle was ready to leave. Caroline was looking sad, and Van knew his mother was thinking the last frail link with Terra was about to snap, leaving them totally alone on a world at the rim of an alien part of their galaxy.

Janna and Hu, the impatient young man who had passed out the supplies, were standing beside the Dome, surrounded by dozens of people who had been strangers but now were friends. Others of the crew were also bidding goodbye, when the shuttle roared and began to move, its thrusters pushing it away from the planet amid flames and dust.

Van felt the shock of it in his stomach, and he turned to look at the people who had been left stranded among these unwilling colonists. Janna had turned white, and Hu was shaking his fists after the disappearing plume that marked the passage of the craft. The other crew members were trembling, crying, gritting their teeth.

Ten thousand people, plus a hundred who had not expected to be among them forever, stood silent, staring at each other, knowing exactly what the Overlords, in their cold way, had done. There were too many people. There were too many trained officers and crews for starships. They were thinning the numbers of every sort of human being in an efficient and heartless manner.

Caroline pushed through the group around Janna. "Come with me, my dear," she said. "You can be one of the Thomases, now. We need another, since we lost Sty. Now we have Janna, and we are nine again."

The girl's neat braids had been whipped by the wind of the craft's takeoff, and her eyes, usually clear and gray-blue, were red-rimmed. But she held herself together, as she took Mama's hand.

"Now I know what you meant, that day you woke. Yes, I will be a Thomas. I am ashamed that I ever served the Overlords in any way." Her jaw clenched, and Van put his arm about her shoulders.

"Nobody could help themselves. Not us. Not you. But now we can, do you realize that? This may not be a pretty world or an easy one to live on, but we have the chance to make the life we want, now. And hang the Overlords!"

About them, other families were taking in new members, who looked as shocked and orphaned as these people had felt when they left their homes to come here. Van realized that if they survived into the future, every new person would provide not only needed skills but also new bloodlines that might carry traits valuable to his kind in the long years to come.

He had never before realized the things he had studied in biology at the state school had real applications for actual people. Now he studied those about him. Besides dark-skinned people like the Thomases, there were families with pale skin and hair, others with coppery faces and brown hair, and still others with the golden hue of Orientals. The more kinds there were, the better their chance of survival, he found himself thinking.

He looked down at Janna. Something similar must have been going through her mind, as well, for she gave a little nod and did not shake his arm from her shoulders as they turned to the Thomases' place in the Dome.

CHAPTER FIVE

Shaking Down

The departure of the shuttle and the ship brought home to Van, as nothing had done before, the actuality of their separation from everything they had ever known or that his studies in school might have prepared him to face. More than ten thousand people, who knew each other slightly if at all, were isolated, without any hope of help from or contact with others of their kind.

They had to learn to survive on this dry gray planet, or every one of them would die. He and his mother and Anthea had talked for a long while about that, with Janna and Hu and Gable, the highest ranking of the officers who had been left behind.

The shock of being abandoned was worse for the crew members, for the deportees had always known they were to be dumped and left. There was anger and there were tears among the abandoned crew. There was depression for a long while among their number, but when Janna found herself a part of his family she shook it off fairly quickly.

Gable, strangely enough, seemed quite content with the state of affairs. When they were sitting in the Thomas home spot, discussing plans for the future, Van ventured to ask him about it.

"It never seemed to bother you much," he said. "I've wondered why. It's none of my business, but I really would like to know if you expected to be marooned here. I thought the ship's officers were pretty close, and it never dawned on me such a thing could happen."

Gable leaned back against the movable wall that gave the family an illusion of privacy. His dark-skinned face was calm, as always, but his brown eyes sparkled as he said, "That is a very good question. Some of my own people have asked the same thing. I think I will tell you...it can't possibly hurt anything now."

Janna leaned forward against Van's shoulder. Since they had become a couple, she seemed to have separated herself, to some extent, from her former shipmates. "Why?" she asked, her tone tense.

The big officer smiled, his teeth white against his dark skin. Warm air circulated about them, as he wrapped his arms around his knees and began.

"I was trained under the old leaders of Terra. We were taught honor and obedience, loyalty and kindness. Those things are ones I had to learn to hide and to deny, once the Overlords came into power on my home world.

"I knew they were dumping millions of people on isolated worlds, too far apart to offer any hope of cooperation, even if, by some miracle, their inhabitants prospered enough to reinvent space travel, over the generations. If you had a ship, here and now, you wouldn't know how to operate it or where to head it even to find Terra, now would you?" He looked around at the others.

Janna shook her head. "The course we were assigned was secret. Only the Navigator and the Captain knew it."

"Exactly. Once that began to be the case, I knew it was only a matter of time until crew would be planeted along with deportees. There are too many trained space-faring people. Once this operation is finished, and at the rate they are going it won't take many years, the Overlords intend to shut down the space service, except for their own limited uses.

"I accessed one of their computers to learn this, strictly illegally, and it's all there. The money they are spending now will come back to them many times over, once that is done.

"Interplanetary trade will die away. The only imported goods will come through the hands of the Overlords, who will make billions, for only those who are well-to-do are going to be left on the worlds of our System. Interplanetary wars will be impossible, for the means will all be in the hands of the Overlords, who know all too well how dangerous that can be to any system of government. After all, it's the way they seized control of our entire sector.

"I watched and waited, as we jumped the warps and set unwilling people on marginal worlds. I knew the time would come when I would be left behind, with any part of the crew that wasn't completely necessary for working the ship.

"This didn't come as a shock or a surprise to me. And that is why I am not depressed or angry. Just relieved, more than anything. The waiting is over."

Caroline touched his big hand. "You have a wonderful attitude." She was mending Sarah's jumpsuit, and her fingers went back to work, but her gaze remained fixed on Gable's face. "Why didn't you warn the others?"

"And have them all upset and worried? That wouldn't be fair to the people they were planeting. No, it's not any worse this way for them than it would have been with warning.

"For me it offers a chance for something different. Something challenging. Something I can, maybe, control or at least help to create."

"You hated the Overlords," Van said, suddenly convinced of that. "And you're glad to be out of their hands, even on this dismal world."

"I am. And this need not be a dismal world, if we keep our heads and work together. We have enough to keep us going for years, if we manage properly. This plain was the best place to set down the shuttle, and that's the reason you are here.

"There is an entire planet out there, with all sorts of terrain. We need not stay here, did you ever think of that? I scanned the screens as we orbited and while they were getting everyone on their feet.

"There is what looks like woodland to the north of here. Deep canyons and sharp ridges run northwest to southeast, south of here, and there seems to be some free water there. We have options, my friends, and if we are wise we will remember it."

"We need not stay here, cramped up with all these people. We might go out and be alone, just our own family, without all the noise and confusion and the constant fighting and quarrelling." Anthea's voice sounded wistful, and her brother remembered suddenly how she had longed, as a child, to go into the farmlands and be one of those assigned to cultivate the crops.

At that moment, a hubbub drowned out her words, as a fight erupted beyond their flimsy wall. Van closed his ears to the obscenities the fighters were yelling, and he suddenly decided what he was going to do, once the situation had shaken down a bit.

"I want to explore," he said, when he could make himself heard. "I want to go out and find what is there, so we can make intelligent choices."

"A good ambition," said Gable. "But it will probably have to wait. There is, as usual, a bunch who intend to run things. They'll have to have their chance to mess up before they will let anybody leave the area of the Dome.

"I heard Flemming and his friends talking today. They intend to form a government and make everybody obey a lot of strict rules." He sighed and stared at Sarah, who was sleeping in Hannah's lap. "Fools," he added in a quiet tone.

Van wondered if he could possibly be right, but the next morning he learned how true the officer's words were. In some way, Flemming and the men and women attached to his family managed to recruit enough others to enforce their demands. As most of the families and individuals were still disoriented and indifferent, that was not difficult.

Those who, like the Thomases, might have objected held their peace. Van wondered who they might be, and if they, too, had a premonition that disaster might follow this step.

But he accepted his assignment when the "elected officials" passed them out. He would, at least, be working beside Janna and Gable at digging up a vegetable garden on the plain behind the Dome. He knew nothing of such things, but he wondered if Terran seeds could sprout here, and if this dry gray soil, which supported only a scanty crop of tan-gray grass, plus some distant scrub of brush, could possibly grow enough food for more than ten thousand mouths.

Caroline was put to tending the smallest children, which suited her very well, and Anthea and Hannah joined a group of young women who were supposed to keep the area sanitary and orderly. That was a task Van didn't envy his sisters, for these were the same people who had made a vast garbage dump of the Blocks, back in City 136.

Yet they all set to work with a will, and before winter set in things had, indeed, begun to shake down fairly well.

Gable, when asked, only grinned. "You will see," he said. "These people can't manage themselves, much less a lot of others. There will be problems they can't handle, and that is the time for us to look for our own ways and take our own roads."

The seeds, of course, never showed their heads, even though it rained frequently enough to give them some sort of chance. The garden was a complete fiasco.

The Dome began to smell like the Blocks back home, a mix of human waste, rotting food, and unwashed people. The well had been laser-drilled, just before the shuttle left, and it supplied plenty of water, but few of the new inhabitants of Heaven had ever washed when water ran from pipes at a touch, in the old homeplace.

Before winter set in, Van was angry and frustrated, ready to take his family out of the Dome, however it could be managed, and creep away into the darkness toward anything that might lie beyond the featureless horizon. The first real blizzard, however, persuaded him his escape would have to wait for spring.

The wind poured over the contours of the land like liquid, carrying with it a harsh sediment of snow. The Dome hummed with the passage of the gusts, the impact of the sleet and the gritty flakes. Those inside, awed and frightened, stopped their incessant quarreling and whining, for a time, appalled at the strength of the storm outside their shelter.

Even as he lay beside Janna in his family's walled quarters, Van was thinking such crowding was dangerous, now that the Dome must be sealed against the weather. He had enjoyed history in school, and he'd heard tapes from the library that told of plagues.

So many people...so many, many germs and viruses...he drifted to sleep thinking of the possibilities that were a part of the situation.

CHAPTER SIX

Grit Your Teeth and Bear It

Although Flemming's deputies did a lot of shouting and beat those who opposed them, it seemed impossible to make the mass of people in the Dome realize they couldn't keep up their bad old ways of doing things. Dirty clothing was not washed. Dirty people got dirtier, and the stench in the Dome became so intolerable that Flemming finally ordered the vents and the door opened twice a day, just to blow out the stench.

The Thomases had always been considered strange because of their clean habits, but all the personal scrubbing with the cleaning agents provided in the shelter, all the washing of their clothing in the water from the well, did nothing to keep the smell of their neighbors from attacking them. Caroline was the first of her family to become ill.

She was not the first of them all, however. By the time she began to run a fever and to feel giddy every time she stood, there were over a hundred people down with the sickness.

Van stood beside his mother's pallet, looking down at her. She stared up, her eyes sunk in her pale face. "I can't live this way, Son," she told him. "I'd rather die than live like a beast in a stinking den."

"I know." He turned to look into Anthea's eyes, and his sister nodded. He sighed.

Gable called from beyond the wall, "May I come?" and Van asked him in, somewhat relieved that the decision he must make was to be postponed for a bit. He knew what his mother wanted, what his older siblings wanted, and it was a dangerous and rash thing.

"I brought you some juice. It isn't the real thing, but I thought it might make you feel better." The big officer held out a cup of amber liquid, the reconstituted powder provided by the Dome's supplies. Rich in vitamins and essential minerals, it had an acid flavor that was somewhat refreshing, and Caroline drank the liquid eagerly.

"Thank you, Frank. You are kind."

She seemed so glad to see Gable that Van gestured for Anthea and Janna to come outside the wall with him and leave the two to talk. The smaller children were playing at the other side of the shelter with a group of their fellows, leaving the place, for once, relatively quiet.

"We've got to get her out of here," Anthea said, nodding toward her mother. "And every one of us is going to get sick, too, if we stay in this place. You know it, Van. I've talked to Hannah, and she agrees. The boys are too little to understand it all, but they're miserable with the noise and the stink."

Janna caught his arm. "I would rather freeze to death in the snow than stay here. It would have been kinder for the Overlords to shoot us all than to stick us out here in this—this animal's den!"

Van knew that, all too well. He had heard bodies being carried out, in the night. When he asked about this, very carefully, he realized that at least a dozen people had died during the hours of darkness, most of them children.

Mark and David and Elton and Sarah were even more at risk than Caroline. She was grown, with a strong body and a lot of resistance. They were vulnerable.

"I understand that. But you know that if we leave the Dome, Flemming is going to make trouble. He may send his men to drag us back." He lowered his voice, as he spoke.

Janna leaned to speak into his ear. "I think not. They're going to be too busy to think about us. I talked with Mrs. Gottschalk, this morning. She said hundreds more are down today. The deputy came and got her husband to go help carry out the dead. When Mr. Gottschalk came back, he said he could see with his own eyes that more and more people are down."

"Then I'll go out, as soon as they open the doors to air out, and see if I can find something to make a shelter. That tent thing—just a part of it would make us something to keep out the wind. Then when they open for the evening air-out, we'll try to get everyone outside."

The decision made, he felt suddenly better. Even freezing to death on the plain was not as frightening as living amid squalor and death and waiting for your turn to fall ill and die.

The two nodded, and turned back to draw aside the curtain and return to Caroline. Van wandered around the narrow aisles that separated the living spaces of the different groups, hearing beyond the fragile walls every sort of noise from deep coughs to helpless giggles.

It seemed a very long time before the vents in the Dome were cracked, high above them, and the wide doors were opened to let the foul air rush out to pollute the plain. As soon as the opening was wide enough, he slipped through, carrying his poncho, which he wrapped tightly around him in the blast of wind.

The doors stayed open for an hour at a time. That should give him the time to find something to set up a windbreak, if nothing else. He staggered through the blast toward a lumpy bulk, which resolved itself into piles of battened-down supplies.

There were lengths of canvas smaller than the large tent he remembered, and that was a help. He had stolen a blade from the cooking equipment bins, but it would have been a long night's work to cut a satisfactory square of material from that huge batch.

Also in the pile of crates and wrappings was a set of bedpacks, and it was easy work to slip out enough for the Thomases. That would keep them from arousing suspicion by taking their own out of their family's space. Another roped heap contained cartons of dried foodstuffs, and he knew they could melt snow for reconstituting it.

He was sweating, even in the cold blast, by the time he had dragged a canvas full of supplies off into the scrub to the north of the Dome. If there was a search for the fugitives, it would likely be aimed at the area sheltered by the bulk of the Dome. He did not intend to be there.

He kept looking backward, using his hand-generated light, to see if he left a track which could be followed. But the constant wind swept the loose dust over the dragged trail as quickly as he made it. He was certain of that, by the time he found a gully, invisible from any distance, that cut through the plain like a scar. This would shelter his people from the wind.

He climbed down carefully and shone his light up and down the walls, which were striped with layers of rocks and soil in different hues, from black to almost orange. There were marks there, too. Water had come down this channel, he thought.

He tried to remember the little he had learned in the geology class his advanced group had taken in school. It came back to him slowly, as he examined the formation of the cut. Of course.

This gully drained the snow water off the plain. When the winter was over and the layer of snow melted, it would be a river. So he needed to find a high place—above that wavering waterline—in which to hide his people.

He had his small chronometer in his pocket, and as he searched, dragging the bulky parcel behind him, he kept track of the time. He had to be back, ready to dart inside, when the doors opened for the morning air-out.

He had found nothing promising; at last he left his burden on a high ledge and retraced his steps to the Dome. Another night or another dozen nights—whatever it took, he intended to find what he was seeking.

Nobody had missed him. When he found himself once again in the Thomas family space, he realized everyone was huddled together, as if to avoid something terrible.

"What's the matter?" he asked Caroline. "I didn't find what we need, but I will. Now why are you all so sad?"

"Mr. and Mrs. Gottschalk are both dying. And three hundred more people are sick. Nobody has survived this, Van. I'm afraid for the children." Her hands were clenched on her everlasting mending, the knuckles white.

Van felt his stomach clench as tightly as her fingers. He had to find a new location for them all, before the plague found a place in their group. Caroline was better—she had evidently had only a stomach virus. But that was sheer luck, and they couldn't count on being lucky again.

He slept all day. Now the Dome was shut for the winter, there was little work to do, and Flemming was no longer so demanding. So when the doors opened again that night Van was once more outside before anyone could see him leave.

This time he was not burdened with the supplies. He sped to the gully and followed it up the country, trying to keep his bearings, though the windings of the cut made him feel as if someone were spinning him around, blindfolded. He left the supplies on their ledge and hurried along, shining his light upward, above the waterline.

He was about to give up, when a dark splotch interrupted the ocher/tan wall above him. It looked big—a cave? He took the rope he had brought from the supply ledge and flipped it upward, again and again, until the hook at its end caught securely. Then he climbed straight up the wall in darkness, unable while climbing to squeeze the light-generator, until he crouched at the opening of a notch in the cliff.

Retrieving his handlight, he sent the beam into the darkness. It went back and back, one side slanting inward, the other outward. But it was solid rock, the roof yards thick, and there was at least as much floor space as his family had in the Dome.

He had found a spot for them to live, while the plague raged in the crowded shelter. With a sigh of relief, he secured the rope to a stub of rock and let himself down again.

He didn't know how and he didn't know exactly when, but his family was about to escape from Flemming and his deputies and the dirty mob inside the Dome.

CHAPTER SEVEN

ESCAPE!

Van barely escaped being detected as he slipped into the Dome again with the morning chill. One of Flemming's deputies opened his bloodshot eyes, just as the young man straightened his back and yawned, after crawling through the space between the door panels.

Luckily, Josh thought he had just come to get a breath of fresh air and nothing came of it, but it made Van cautious. "We have to wait for a couple of days, until they are so busy they won't notice anything. Then we'll all go, one by one, and slide out through the space. That shouldn't be so hard."

He was wrong, of course. As more and more of the people sickened and died, Flemming grew desperate and irrational. He seemed to feel the deportees were dying just to spite him.

Gable watched the self-styled leader closely and came often to talk with the Thomases, as the days passed. At last Van confided in the big fellow what he planned to do. He was half afraid to do it, but he found to his astonishment that the officer was ready to go with them.

"This is a bad thing, here," Gable said, frowning. "Flemming is losing control of himself, and that means he'll lose control of his deputies pretty soon. Then we'll have all sorts of abuses. Not to mention the fact that the sickness is getting worse. Nothing in the stores of medicine seems to affect it at all. So if you'll have me, I'd like to go."

He had asked Van, but the boy noticed he was actually watching Caroline out of the corner of his eye. She nodded slightly, and her son felt a vast relief.

"Glad to have you," he said softly. "And when do you think we should make the attempt?"

"Tonight."

That surprised Van. He had thought the older man would want to be more cautious, but Gable put a hand on his arm and shook it gently for emphasis.

"Every day, every night, more people get sick. We have lost four hundred and fifty, now. You may not know it—they didn't train you people to survive here, I know—but this Dome will remain heated only while there are at least five thousand warm bodies living here.

"Once the number drops below that, the heating system will not be activated. And then anyone who has already gone out and found a way to live with this world is going to be a long way ahead of the rest."

Van felt shock go through him. "But that's stupid!" he said. "Didn't they understand a lot of us might die off or leave the Dome?"

"They didn't care, boy," the officer said. He leaned his dark head against the post holding up their wall. "And they thought, I believe, that if your numbers dropped so far you might as well all freeze at once as linger on and die a few at a time."

Caroline hissed, and they began talking of family matters as a deputy wandered past. He looked stunned...so much so that Gable rose and touched his shoulder. "What's wrong, Josh?"

The man stared up at the big officer, his face blank with shock. "Flemming—he just—he just died."

"But he wasn't sick!" Gable protested.

"It wasn't the plague. His heart, I think. He just keeled over, right up there." He pointed toward the platform Flemming had caused to be built, in order to give those on the floor level more room.

"Too bad," said Gable, but when he turned to look at Van, he looked diabolically cheerful.

"Tonight!" he said again, when the deputy had wandered out of sight.

The doors were opened from force of habit, without Flemming's bellowed order. Then, while the Dome full of bewildered people buzzed with speculation, the Thomas family, along with Gable and Janna, crept through the crack between the door leaves and made their way off into the darkness.

Van led the way, squeezing and releasing his hand-generated light with one hand and carrying his LCF staff in the other. The others saved their lights, for while the generators lasted a long time, the bulbs would eventually burn out. There could be no replacements.

The three staffs carried by Caroline, Van, Anthea, and Gable would last for generations. The boy comforted himself with the knowledge that if they ran into dangerous beasts they would have weapons for protection.

The gully was dark, its bottom slick with snow and ice. Van stood below, shining his light upward as Gable helped the others climb down the rough wall of the cleft. The rock shone with frosty moisture, and the wind whistled overhead, humming over the lip of the ravine with an eerie moan.

Van felt himself chilling with more than the cold of the night. The small boys looked terribly pale and vulnerable, their small faces white patches against the rock, their hands clinging desperately to the ropes Van had brought to make the descent more secure. Sarah rode Gable's back and would come down with him, but his mother and the two girls slid downward, their feet bouncing from the wall awkwardly as they followed Gable's instructions.

"Rappel! Rappel! Remember the way I told you!" the big fellow called from the top, as Caroline slammed painfully against a knee of rock.

She grunted as she dropped to stand beside her daughters and Van. "I wonder...are we doing the right thing?" She gazed upward at the small boys, still hanging onto their own ropes and moving downward.

Once the entire group had reached the bottom, out of the icy wind, everyone felt better. Van started off with a light at the head of the line, and Gable came behind, keeping an eye on the small ones. Sarah, sitting on his shoulders, shouted directions and giggled.

Even out of the wind, the air was freezing, with a dead chill that numbed the hands and feet. The all-weather ponchos, which kept the body's heat inside their folds, helped, but any part that was outside became painful very quickly.

"It's not too far, now," Van called back, as he approached a dogleg bend he recalled as being very near the cave. He rounded the angle and shone his light along the way. The dark smudge that was the mouth of the opening showed in the ice-shiny wall of the cleft. His family had come to the end of this miserable journey.

The rope he had left hanging was now frozen to the rock wall in a sheath of ice. Van focused a beam of energy on a nearby span. The LCF did not make heat, itself, but if it excited the molecules of the rock for long enough, that action generated heat of its own. Soon the rope was free, allowing Gable to climb it.

"I'm the largest. I can pull the others up, if they need help. You stay down here and help the little ones," he said to Van, offloading Sarah onto her brother's back.

He tucked his staff into its sling, which he had made and attached to his belt. Then he went up, quickly and easily, looking like a great dark spider against the shiny rock. The rope jerked loose from its frozen position as he moved, and when he reached the top and crawled into the cave, he gave it a reassuring jerk.

Caroline tied on the ends of the other ropes and flipped the line. The bunch began to rise up the cliff, and they all waited impatiently until Gable's dark hand came into view, grasping the bundle and pulling the ends into the hole. Here was a short wait while he secured the ends to rocks inside the shelter, and then a loose gaggle of free ends came whipping down again.

"Come on, Mark. You put David ahead of you and start up. I'm down here to catch you, if you fall, and Gable will pull you, if you get too tired to climb. Shoo!" Caroline started the boys up a pair of lines and turned to secure Anthea and Hannah to theirs.

When Elton balked at the idea of going up the cliff alone, Caroline went up with him, carrying him on her back. That left Van to come behind with Sarah. Janna followed as if used to such exercises, for which she probably had been trained in the space service. In less than an hour they were all crowded into their quarters, along with the new supplies he had brought from the dump.

There was no time to rest. As soon as the least ones were secure, the older ones and Gable went out again, this time climbing the wall to the plain above their heads. That was only a dozen or so yards farther up, and they found themselves out in the cutting wind sooner than they liked.

Fuel had to be brought, however, for the cave was as cold as the gully, and they had to have heat. Fortunately, the plain was overgrown with large tracts of scrubby brush, which seemed dry enough to kindle, even with the coat of ice that made it as brittle as glass.

They gathered huge bundles of the stuff and tied them with the handy cords. When there were as many as each of them could drag, they started back, arriving at the cave well before daybreak, when the edge of the sky was only beginning to pale a bit. Again, the sweeping wind obliterated their tracks as they moved, making it impossible for anyone searching to find their hideout.

They found the children sleeping, the bed packs put together so they could cuddle together and share their warmth. Caroline had lain down with them, spreading all their ponchos over the group to keep them warm. Even so, her face was pinched with chill as she crawled out to help the others build a fire.

Until arriving on this new world, Van had never even seen open flame. Creating a fire from the ice-coated branches and twigs they had gleaned seemed something too difficult to attempt, but Gable seemed to know just how to go about it.

Using his LCF on the pile he had arranged in careful layers, he played the beam over the heap for a long while, sweeping it in regular rhythm, back and forth. In time, the gray wood began to drop its sheathing of ice, and the bark beneath grew dry.

Van helped his mother and Anthea take away the chunks of ice and throw them down into the gully, to keep the stuff from melting and drowning out their fire-to-be. When at last Gable was ready to light the gray mass, Van watched, fascinated, as the officer took from his pocket a small Flamer. He had never thought of a weapon as something with which to kindle a fire, but now he saw the blue blaze lick over the wood, which began to crackle and spark almost at once.

The fire leaped high, filling the cave with its ruddy light, and the dry scent of smoke made everyone cough. But they laughed as they coughed, for this seemed more cheerful and comforting than anything that had happened since they arrived on this alien world the Overlords had called Heaven.

Gable rose from his haunches. "Get that piece of canvas, Van," he said. "We need to close up our front door, so the light can't show from outside. If they look for us, it will give us away."

"What about the smoke?" asked Caroline, pulling at one side of the big piece of tent material, so Gable could sear it into shape with his Flamer. "We'll smother in here, if it can't get out." She coughed again.

"I'll leave a crack, up near the top where the overhang of rock will shield the light. Come, now. Heave!"

The three of them hauled the impervious material into position and secured it against the rock, stacking boxes against it to hold it in place. When that was done, a room some thirty feet long and twelve wide, at its widest, was enclosed, snug and bright and far more homelike than the Dome had ever been.

And that was the precise moment when Van heard a growl.

CHAPTER EIGHT

The Gurry-Hound

Everyone froze in place. Van glanced desperately about, but his own LCF was lying beside small Sarah's sleeping place, and Gable's was on the other side of the cave. He couldn't see his mother's.

The noise at the back of the cave was coming closer, a snarling sounding almost like words—"Gurrr-eee! Gurrr-eee!" The click of toenails on stone made Van's skin crawl, as he moved at last toward his staff, which was some yards down the length of the cave.

Before he could reach it, there was a rush of paws, a gust of stink, and a hound-like shape came bounding into the room, between the group of sleeping children and their appalled elders. It came to a halt, its narrow head up, its yellow eyes staring first at the fire, then at the intruders into its home.

Neither seemed to frighten it. Van saw the hair between its high shoulder blades rise into a coarse ridge, its mouth open wider, allowing its double row of teeth to glisten in the firelight. Then the thing was on top of him, and he was fighting for his life.

Holding the foul head away from his face with all the strength in his arms, the boy tried to roll, to kick, to work himself free of his attacker, whose hind claws were raking his legs like blades. Gable was on top of the beast, now, his dark hands around its throat, but even his great strength could not affect the animal.

There came a small voice into the panting and snuffling and grunting that filled the cave. "Move away. I'll get him."

Van felt his skin creep. It was Anthea.

But Gable rolled aside at once. Beneath the scruffy side of the beast, Van watched as his younger sister took the staff, twisted the control ring as she had been taught, and aimed it at the thing on top of him.

The creature shrieked and its body convulsed. The smell of blood and entrails filled the place, as Van was able to pull away from the beast now rolling on the stony floor, clawing at its back, flinging its head from side to side in agony.

Caroline took the staff from her daughter and aimed the flame, invisible in the red firelight, at the creature's brain. The agonized movements ended, and the animal lay still in the midst of the room they now called home.

Again Anthea spoke, her voice troubled. "This was its home. I did have to kill it, didn't I? It would have hurt Van, if I hadn't." She sounded as if she might cry.

Caroline twisted the ring to deactivate the LCF and leaned the staff again against the wall. Then she took Anthea into her arms and held her close.

It was Gable who spoke. "You did have to kill it, my dear. It would have killed Van and, perhaps, more of us, too. It is too bad. We didn't intend for this to happen, but as it has, we just have to understand it was necessary. All right?"

He held out his arms to her, and she went from her mother to this large man who had become so close to her family. She buried her face in his shoulder, and Van nodded as Gable's gaze met his own. "I'm sorry to be such a sissy," the girl murmured. "Forgive me!"

Caroline was examining his cuts and bruises, already, her medical kit, which she had put together from supplies found at the dump, open for use. Stinging stuff went into all the cuts, and Van winced as she wrapped the plastiskin about his bitten wrists and scraped legs, which the creature's back claws had almost skinned.

When she was through with him, she looked at Gable's hands, which had also suffered. Sarah climbed gingerly into her brother's lap and watched while her mother bandaged Gable, too. She giggled when she looked at the small boys, who still slept peacefully, having missed all the excitement.

"Anthea killed that Gurry-hound," she said to Van, turning her face up to his. "Didn't she?"

He nodded. "She did, indeed, and you didn't cry or make a sound. I think you will be a wonderful Pioneer Woman, Sarah, if you can do that."

Before the winter was over, however, Van wondered if any of them would survive, far less become pioneers. The cold seemed unending. The dump of supplies dwindled rapidly, as he could tell when he went for more food and equipment for his family.

Worse yet, the frozen bodies, lined up in stacked walls on the southern side of the Dome, grew more and more numerous. At last he asked Gable to come with him on a food-run, in order to help him estimate the number of living people who might be left in the Dome.

While he filled his canvas carryall with packets of food, the big officer walked up and down the rows of the dead. From time to time, he would find a sheltered spot and activate his hand torch, and in its light Van could see his face, drawn with grief. When he turned to rejoin his companion, he walked like an old man, his steps weary and his shoulders hunched.

"I think there must be more than fifteen hundred dead there, now. There won't be enough people left to keep the Dome warm, by spring. Maybe, if something doesn't change, there won't be enough to keep a nucleus of our kind surviving on this world.

"We need to find something, Van. Something that will give us an edge, so we can live with this world, rather than camping out on it."

Van knew he was right. As they tramped through the skimpy snow back to the cave, checking constantly to see that the wind swept their tracks away, he thought of the man's words. When spring came...when the weather cleared enough to allow him to walk across the Plain without freezing, he would go northward and examine those gray forests he had seen from orbit. Whatever was there, it could not be worse than the country around the Dome.

When, at long last, the time came for him to start out, he found himself wondering if he might be foolish. The Plain stretched, seemingly endlessly, to the north, and days of walking seemed not to change any of the scenery around him.

The sky still ran down to weld itself to the undulating horizon. The gray-tan soil, only lightly covered with pale greeny-tan grass, held what seemed to be the same clumps of scrub, whose bleached leaf-buds were only beginning to open into narrow clusters.

The gully ran northwestward, and Gable had assured him that the shortest distance to the treed lands was due north, so he had no ready source of water. He hoped the canisters hung about his waist would hold enough to see him to his goal and that once there he would find more to get him home again.

Yet he refused to worry. He had to try, for if he did not, then Gable must go, and he knew the officer would be far more help, remaining with his family, than he ever could.

He had been walking since dawn, his eyes scanning the horizon without really seeing it. Suddenly, as the sun reached the halfway point in the eastern sky, he realized he was seeing something that was not the normal Plains contour. Something gray and uneven rose at the edge of his vision, and he hurried forward, going up and down the slow rolls of the land, trying to make that edge come nearer.

By mid-afternoon, he could see the grayish haze of trees standing at the edge of the Plain. He camped reluctantly, wanting to keep pushing ahead to find the forest he had waited so long to see. He knew that would be foolish, and he stopped, ate and drank sparingly, and rolled in his poncho for the night.

He woke before dawn to stare into the cloudless depths. The stars were few but very bright, with no moon to dull their impact, and he watched them pale as the light touched the sky in the east. He was on his feet at once, rolling his poncho, for when the cold wind stopped blowing the Plain became more than warm as soon as the sun rose.

Then he sped onward, refreshed by his rest, spurred by his need to reach that forest, which now began to be visible as individual trees, scanty enough, but the first he had seen since they left his Block and its lone oak tree. Even as he hurried, a wind rose again from the northwest, whipping the warmth from the land and forcing him to pause and don his poncho again. A late snowstorm seemed bent upon delaying him, even within sight of his goal.

Snow began to sting his cheeks, and by the time he reached the fringe of the forest the soil had chilled enough to hold patches of mixed snow and sleet. He moved under the first trees, finding to his relief that the bulk of the wood ahead of him broke the force of the wind.

Reassured, he forged ahead, finding the growth thicker the farther he went. He camped that night beside a roaring fire, for Gable had insisted that he take the Flamer, as well as his own staff. Kindling the deadfall he found under the trees was easy, using such concentrated heat. When he sat in the shelter of a thicket with his own blaze before him and his food packet warmed in the ashes at its edge, he felt strangely triumphant.

If nothing else, this place would shelter and warm his people. Surely there would be food animals, perhaps plants that would be edible, if the Thomases could find what they were. Hope, which had become thin and distant during the winter months, sprouted in his heart, and he slept beside the coals of his fire and dreamed of good times to come.

CHAPTER NINE

THE GREIST

When he woke, his poncho was covered with snow, and the trees around his tiny clearing were outlined with white along their dark branches. Somewhere in the distance an animal was bellowing. He had never heard a cow, but he thought one might sound something like that.

This gave him even more hope, for although he knew nothing about livestock, he suspected Gable did. The big officer seemed to have a fund of useful skills at his fingertips. Taming wild animals to raise for their skins and meat might well be one of them.

He did not rekindle the fire, for he had enough common sense to know that wildfire in a forest would not be a good thing for anyone. Instead, he scraped snow to cover the last of the embers, hearing them spit and sputter as they died to black ash.

Then he turned his face to the north again, holding the slanting light from the half-obscured sun on his right, and trudged through the snow. Even as he went, he heard the bellowing again, along with other sounds—chirps and twitters as if birds lived in these gray trees, small grunts and chitterings as of small animals burrowed into the floor of the forest.

It was cold. The warm days of the past week might never have been, though the stiff branches above his head held small grayish buds promising to become leaves, in time. He found himself climbing. Not a swell, this time, but a true hill, which he conquered at last, to find himself looking down a steep slope toward the chuckle of a running stream, hidden among brush at its bottom.

He felt his canisters at his waist, very light now: dangerously light, if it were not for the snow. But if he could refill them at the stream, hang them in a tree for retrieving when he returned, he would know he could get home alive. Drinkable water had been one of the things the Overlords required of the worlds where they dumped excess population.

He ran down the hill, his equipment banging and jangling about him, and found the trickle of water running among stones, its edges frozen into jagged edges of ice. On his knees, he held the canisters, one by one, beneath a small waterfall and let them fill. This was his insurance that he would live to bring his people here.

They could use logs to build houses, he thought. Wood to build fires. Stone, which he could see as gray outcrops among the tree roots, for other building. This was a country in which people could live, if they knew how—or if they could learn quickly enough.

He tied the containers to the branches of a leaning tree, using the yellow scarf he had found among the supplies to mark the spot. With that beacon to signal him, he felt he could find the place again, easily enough.

Unburdened of the weight, he sprang forward, across the brook and up the even higher hill beyond it. It was the first of many such hills, and at the top of each he made an arrow of fallen branches, pointing the way back to his water supply.

In time, he stopped more often to make his signs at points where he had to go around dense growths of trees and bushes or to avoid other streams too wide and deep to jump across. But always he found a way at last, going northward as nearly as he could.

It was almost dark when he came to a great valley filled with trees larger than any he had seen, so far. The sky was darkening, as much with snow clouds as with the coming of night, and he shivered. Even a fire and a thicket at his back seemed insufficient to counter the icy breeze that fingered its way among the interlocked branches to find him and probe through his trousers and his poncho.

He needed a spot with a rocky outcrop to windward, he decided, and kept going, using his hand-light when the sky grew completely dark. Then he felt a subtle warmth against his face.

It was not the warmth of fire, or even the disturbing sensation that was not quite heat that the LCF supplied. It was a...a furry warmth. As well, something seemed to be murmuring into his mind, "Come! Oh, come!"

He followed the feeling, using his light only when he got caught in a tangle, until he stood at the edge of a clear space some fifty feet in circumference. The delightful warmth seemed to rise from that space, though in the dim light it seemed to be covered with a particularly odd-looking sort of grass.

There was no sign of anything capable of speaking to him, but he went forward still, called by something that found an echo inside his own mind. A wonderful warmth rose up through the soles of his boots, and his toes welcomed it. He sat on the grass to take off his footgear, and when his bottom touched the grass he found it irresistible. He had to lie flat, turn on his face, and bury his ear in the comfort of thick and yet strangely silky strands.

The patch of grassy stuff was alive, it was instantly apparent. The grass was fur, and the heat came from the life processes in that great flat body. Beneath his ear, there was a muffled throb, as of a huge heart beating, sending some blood-like substance pulsing through a large and friendly beast.

"I am the Greist."

The words did not come to his ear—not exactly. They came into his mind, not quite in words; yet in some way he understood perfectly clearly.

"I have needed small ones to lie on my fur, to listen to my stories, to feel with me the wonders of the world. Welcome, Small One. Welcome."

It was as much an emotion as an idea. Van felt as if he had come home, after a long time away, to find his family waiting for him with their arms outstretched and smiles on their faces. This great creature had been so lonely; the remnant of isolation clung about it still, so that the feeling almost chilled him, even in the midst of his pleasure.

"There are more of us," he murmured into the furry mat. "Many more. Families who need to come here and live. You are too small to warm them all, big though you are."

The thing was quiet for a long time, and Van dozed, more comfortable than he had been since he could remember. Then it woke him with more thoughts, trickling into his mind.

"There are many Greist. We live for long and long—two smaller kinds were once upon this world. They lived their cycles and died away, leaving us alone, with memories of them and their ways, and yet with no one to tell the stories to.

"Many valleys contain my kind. If there is need for us again, we will all be glad, for Greist do not need Greist. We need Small Ones to comfort and to teach."

"Teach?" The question brought Van upright. Remembering, he lay down again, putting his ear to the fur. "Can you teach us how to live on this world? We are not skilled at survival on any world at all, and we need to learn everything about this one. What we can eat and how we can find animals we can tame and how to build shelters. Few of us know such things, if any at all do. You can, truly, teach us?"

"I can," came the reply. "Oh, I can!" And while there could be no tone to words that were not really words and had no voice, Van thought he felt joy all through the creature upon which he lay. Something much like a purr vibrated the fur beneath his body.

He sighed and closed his eyes. Stories of strange beings, busy with stranger lives, spun into his dreams. He slept deeply, and when he woke he knew he had found what was necessary to allow those who still lived on this new world to survive and even, perhaps, to prosper here.

At the very least, the Thomases and Janna and Gable would live and grow and multiply, he was certain. With that thought in mind, he turned away from his own Greist, knowing he could find it again. A link had been forged between them that would guide him truly, when he brought his family back to this welcoming creature and the sheltering gray-oak forest.

A PLANET CALLED HEAVEN, BY ARDATH MAYHAR

PART TWO

AWAY FROM THE GRAY-OAK

A PLANET CALLED HEAVEN, BY ARDATH MAYHAR

CHAPTER TEN

Time Flies

A thousand years went past. Those who had followed Van Thomas to the forest lived, most of them, and reared their children and learned from the Greist the way in which to live on this world, which certainly was not much like Heaven.

Those remaining behind in the Dome were too few to keep it warm. In time they, too, came to the Gray-Oak Hills and found their own Greist and a way to live with some comfort and dignity.

The Dome stood empty, and the winds whined through it; the stores remained, waiting for hungry mouths that never came. The world on which the deportees now lived provided animals for meat and milk, plants for food, and a life that was far cleaner and less filled with anger than the one their ancestors had left behind on old Terra.

Yet nothing ever remains the same. And no living thing lives forever. Not even the Greist.

CHAPTER ELEVEN

The Greist Is Dead!

As she reached the lip of the home glen, Hanne could see the tall shape of her grandfather standing beside the campfire that blazed before the summer yurt. Already he had the shafts hooked onto the yoke, ready to strap to the necks of the boar-oxen for the trip to the wintering place.

Her small brother, Tomba, was beneath the contraption, half-hidden by the flaps of fabric forming its walls. He was evidently making a last adjustment to the load beneath the awkward vehicle, for his grubby legs were sticking out from the skirting, often waving wildly. Her grandfather had grown too stiff to crawl about, now, and she and Tomba had to do many things they were almost too small to accomplish.

She sighed. They were ready to move to the winter camp, only waiting for her to return with the present location of their family's Greist before they broke camp and began the long slow journey to its position. Hanne's breath caught in a hard jolt. Tears rose into her eyes, though she dashed them away impatiently.

Clutching her small staff, with its tiny glint of the Holy Fire in the cup at its end, she began to scramble down the slope to the stream trickling past the yurt. Her grandfather heard her call. He raised his head, and she knew his sharp eyes noted her haste and the stiff set of her body as she moved.

He took his own fire-staff from its place beside the yurt and strode to meet her. Crossing the stream with a long sure step, he moved swiftly up the slope.

Before he reached her, she could bear it no longer and cried out, "Granda! Oh, Granda! The Greist is dead! I found him in a gray-oak copse, beyond the Hill of the Healers, and he was weak and filled with pain. When I lay on him and stroked him, there was no warmth, only shivering."

"Shhh, Child. Shhh!" her grandfather soothed her. He lifted her in his thin arms and carried her back toward the camp. "There is no hurry, Hanne. Tell us slowly, after you have eaten and drunk. You are thin and almost fevered, yourself."

"Tomba!" he called, as they reached the stream. The legs scrabbled backward until the whole of the boy emerged from beneath the yurt.

"Pour tea for your sister and cut a bit of the oat bread and the cheese."

Though Tomba hated waiting on anyone, and Hanne in particular, he did as his grandfather asked. Hanne was almost cheered at seeing him so subdued, and the food did seem to warm her a bit.

When she sat at last beside the family's yurt, fed and her terrible thirst quenched, she found the traitorous tears forming again behind her eyes. She drew a deep breath, fighting for control.

Then she said, "How can we live, Granda, without a Greist to lie beneath our camp and warm a spot for us during the winter? How can we bear the long, cold days, the loneliness while the snow traps us in place, without his winter tales forming in our minds? There is no family in all the Gray-Oak Hills without a Greist. We will die!"

Her grandfather shook his head, his grizzled hair moving in the light breeze from the north. "Our kind did not always have the Greist to lie beneath his winter camps and tell us tales while the snows fell," he replied.

"When my ancestors came on the great Ship, with those of the other Families, it was the way of our kind to make our own way, with tools and our hands and the help of the Holy Fire. The first winter on this world was terrible, and few were left after it ended. The Ship had gone, not to return for generations, if ever. No help could be hoped for, and they almost despaired as another winter approached."

Thom sighed and stared away over the tops of the misty gray oak trees. "My own ancestor found the first of the Greist, lying in its winter spot. He had the wit not to fear the great flat creature, like a rug of grassy fur or of furry grass. It warmed the soles of his feet and stretched and filled with joy when he touched it with his hands." He smiled at his grandchildren, and Hanne found herself comforted, despite her worry.

"It was he who had the courage to lie upon that Greist, to bury his face in its aromatic fur, and to receive the very first words a Greist formed into the mind of a man. He knew, then, his kind could survive on this new and inhospitable world. There was help, though not of any kind we had ever known before."

Tomba crept up to stand within the circle of Thom's arm, listening. No matter how often the tale was told, the children loved to hear it again.

"He returned and told his companions to hunt the Gray-Oak from end to end, until every family had a Greist to warm their winter camp underfoot, keeping away the snow, and to comfort the hearts of his children with its tales. They did not believe, until he led his own family to his discovery, which he claimed for them, as long as the Greist agreed.

"Those who followed, fearful of the plague that was killing them by the hundreds, found many of the creatures, and they discovered the Greist were lonely. For ages and ages, they had lived on this world, missing the days when they were young and traveled over the entire continent, learning as they went and communicating with the kinds of creatures that lived here, long ago.

"As they aged, they told our ancestors, there came into being a race that was young, in its turn. They learned to live with them, to comfort them, and to tell the tales of their wanderings to them, as well as other stories they created in their own strange minds."

He paused, his own eyes dim with tears. "Tell us, now, Hanne. How did our own dear Greist die?"

She blinked hard. "He was very ill, Granda, when I came. I asked if I should travel after you, for I thought you might have medicines in your bag that could help a dying

Greist. But he asked me to lie down on him and think with him for one last time.

"He told me many things—I can't remember them all. But most of all he told me how lonely he had been until our sort came. The beings who used to live here were his companions, and many of the tales he told to us were made for them.

"Then they died away, leaving him alone, and he never knew quite why they went. It comforted his age, he said, to have new young ones to think with, for all these years.

"And then he told me to take a bit of his fur—a good handful. I have it in my pouch, this minute. He said that though Greist live for a long, long time, at last even they must die. All of the Greist in the Gray-Oak are reaching the end of their time, and within a few turnings of the year, they, too, will die.

"We must plant his fur, one strand at a time, beneath stones, against the soil, when we find a safe place in which to winter. More Greist will grow from it, in time, though the time may be very long."

Thom gazed toward the lip of the glen, which was shadowed with the coming of night. "And then he died," he said, his tone almost lost in the breeze.

Hanne nodded. "He was gone, just like that. His fur was suddenly stiff and dry, and there was no feel of tingling life in his big flat body."

Her grandfather sighed. "Then we must move away, my children. I promised, when your father was killed by the Gurry-hound and your mother was caught by the creep-vine, that I would rear you both until you were grown. I intend to do it, though that may seem impossible without our Greist to warm our winter camp and keep growing things tender and edible beneath his fur.

"We must head southward, as quickly as possible. There is warmer weather there, though little else to sustain our kind."

"Away from the Gray Oak Hills?" gasped Hanne. Tomba echoed her words.

Thom nodded. "Catch the boar-oxen, Hanne. Halter their calf to the tail of the yurt. Tomba, make sure all of our bags of foodstuffs, the dried fruits, the acorn-nuts, the herbs, are stored safely.

"We must travel tonight, as far as the beasts can go before they weary. This breeze smells of snow, and there are few days left to us before it flies. I will cover the fire beneath the pot. I will prepare the Holy Fire to travel, as well." He closed his eyes for a moment, and Hanne could see weariness in him, and sadness, and a despairing sort of courage.

"Hurry!" he said. "Hurry!"

CHAPTER TWELVE

The Journey

Darkness came down over the hills, and a brilliant band of stars bloomed from north to south, making the rest of the sky seem blacker in its emptiness. They gave a fair light for the journey, for they were brilliant: great suns hanging in distant spaces in this lonely arm of the galaxy.

Thom placed the staff with its canister of Holy Fire, covered with its gleaming cap of strange metal, on its rack at the front of the yurt. The undying flame was turned very low, to quiet its energies and save its strength for future needs. Thom walked between the boar-oxen, tending them and watching the Fire. Only that was left to humankind on this world, of all the many technologies their kind had known, and it was the duty of the family leader to see it came to no harm.

Hanne and Tomba came behind, watching the yurt, seeing that no flap of fabric or hanging bundle fell and was lost. No matter how carefully you fastened your possessions to a yurt, the constant motion was always loosing a knot or a loop and letting something fall.

Hanne found herself looking back, from time to time, as they made their way through the hills. Never in all her short life had she or any she knew left the haven of the Gray-Oak Hills. Every step left her feeling more exposed to dangers she could hardly imagine.

"Hanne! Granda!" The cry was choked off, but it was Tomba's voice.

She ran forward to the struggling shape that lay on the track of the yurt, wondering why her brother had fallen and what made him wriggle so desperately.

"Tomba? What is it?"

The boy's fingers were fixed into something wound about his neck. "Can't talk," he gasped. She could see that both his hands were strained to the utmost, trying to pull the thing off before it choked him.

Thom was coming, now, leaving the beasts standing. His fire-staff lit the scanty oaks about them to a gray mist, as he neared them. By the light, Hanne could see something like a rope. When she touched it, it seemed warm, and it pulsed with life.

It went around Tomba's neck several times, and her tugging did not loosen its grip. Tomba was turning purple, as her grandfather bent over him.

"It's choking him, Granda," she said, still pulling at the ridged strand. "Make it come loose, can you?"

Thom stooped closer yet, staring at the creature. Then he ran a gentle finger down its length in a tickling motion. At once, the creature relaxed, allowing the old man to draw its length away from Tomba's bruised throat.

Thom helped Tomba to his feet. "Did it hurt you?" he asked. "Or did it merely frighten you?"

Tomba, still rubbing his neck, looked thoughtful. "Well, it scared me more than anything. I was walking along, and suddenly it had me, going tighter and tighter."

"It fell from that branch up there." Thom pointed toward a low-hanging limb, just high enough to clear the top of the yurt. "It let itself fall, I suspect, because it was curious; you were frightened, so it became frightened, too.

"This, like the Greist, is an empath, and it feels what you feel. It is a constrictor, so it squeezed, but as an empath, it can only squeeze hard enough to kill when it is completely desperate, for it hurts itself, literally, as much as it does you."

"But what is it, Granda?" Hanne asked, staring at the twisty length that moved sinuously in the light of the staff.

"A Taffte. They make excellent pets, or so I have been told. As we have no Greist, now, perhaps we might take the Taffte with us to our new home. It will be happy, if we allow it to burrow into the ground from time to time after its natural food. Without the Greist's tales to interest us through the winter, we may find this little creature a source of amusement."

So the Taffte went with them through the star-banded night, and they traveled a very long, slow distance before the boar-oxen grew weary. When they went to their blankets at last, safe in the depths of the yurt, Hanne and Tomba slept at once, but Hanne knew, even as she drifted off, that Thom would sit for a long while at the flap of the shelter, gazing across the invisible miles ahead. He worried, she knew.

When she woke, the Taffte was curled around her arm, warming both her and itself and pulsing gently with a soothing rhythm. It cheered her, somehow, as she made ready for the day ahead.

That day they found themselves at the edge of the Gray-Oak Hills, facing a seemingly endless plain, which flowed in every possible shade of gray and tan and ochre to the horizon. Hanne, who had lived her life surrounded by hills and the forest of oaks, was astonished and frightened by the country through which they must travel.

"Granda," she said, tugging at his shawl, "Must we go out into that? If we went to the other families, they would share with us. We could manage to survive."

Thom put his hand on her head and patted it softly. "Not as a family, Hanne. No single group could take us all...we would have to be shared out among three. They would never begrudge us warmth and space, but we would grow into other families and out of our own. Our ancestors learned families are very important. The Family Thomas must survive together."

Hanne sighed and trudged after the yurt, whose heavy wheels were crossing the last slope of the very last hill. And then they were cutting into the gray-tan grasses of the plain. She turned and looked longingly at the familiar country behind her, but the wheels moved on, and she must follow them.

It had seemed they moved quickly, when there were trees and hills to slide past and recede into the distance. Now they seemed to go impossibly slowly. The horizon never came nearer, and the hills behind them shrank slowly to a dim line that never seemed to change.

When they stopped to rest the animals and to prepare food, the hills still watched them. It was only when they made their night camp, long after the sun had set, that the line of gray was lost over the edge of this new grass-grown world.

The Holy Fire, so familiar they never noticed it consciously when they were in their own familiar surroundings, now glowed with a blue-white vigor inside the yurt. Freed from its impervious container, its energies made Hanne's hair prickle at the roots, and her nerves crawled and twitched. The heatless light made everything in the shelter stand out sharply. She was glad when Thom charged his staff at the glow, for use as a torch, and went outside to kindle a cook fire, using the hastily gathered wood they had brought from the oak forest.

As soon as the pot boiled, they made herb tea, which they drank with their meal of roasted acorn-nuts and toasted bits of oaten bread. When they had finished and washed their few utensils, Thom drew from a pouch at his side a very worn book. He smoothed a square of trampled soil and chose two splinters from the small pile of firewood.

Hanne watched with a mixture of disgust and anticipation. He was getting ready to give them their lessons, though she had fully expected to leave those behind with the Gray Oak Hills. The teacher was far away, now, but her grandfather would, she knew, continue their lessons without interruption.

Her grandfather looked up, a twinkle in his eyes. "No teacher will be with us, this winter, to instruct you while I go about trying to cure the sick. There is nothing for it but to make do with the things I can teach you, myself." He began to trace letters into the soil.

Some few of the survivors of the trek had known the forbidden art of reading, and they had taught others, until no family now living upon this world lacked someone who could write and read messages from others. That skill had been a matter of survival for their descendants, when dangers came or weather threatened.

While the cook fire flickered in its ring of heaped soil, which prevented the sparks from catching the dry grass of the plain, the children copied their letters and did sums and recited the history of their kind on this world that a bored bureaucrat in another system had called Heaven. This was not what the present tenants called it, of course. Their ancestors had found its name was a cruel joke, and those born later were too busy at surviving to worry about such unimportant matters.

Hanne was neither fearful nor bitter, however. History was merely an unpleasant chore, to be gone through as quickly as possible. She wondered if her ancestors had written this thick book simply to burden their grandchildren.

"Finding the inner worlds sadly overcrowded," Tomba quoted by rote from the book. "The Council of Overlords looked to the suns at the edge of their galaxy for planets on which to deposit unwanted people. Large carrier-ships were built and orbited, and entire communities of human beings were placed there for transport in frozen sleep, their ranks balanced carefully for skills, racial heritage, and mental capacities."

There he faltered, and Hanne took up the tale: "Each community was then deposited upon a world deemed to be habitable, to some degree, for our kind. A minimum of equipment was left with each colony, as it was felt necessity would drive them to learn to live in the new systems more quickly than they would if well supplied with survival supplies. Much expense was thereby spared...." Her gray eyes opened wide as the sense of what she had said awoke her mind to alertness.

"Granda, they didn't care!" she exclaimed. "They put our people down on this world and went away and said maybe they would come back and maybe not. They didn't care about the Gurries or the creep-vines or the Silent Suckers or the terrible winters. They hoped...they hoped we would all die, didn't they?"

Her grandfather looked both grim and sad. "I have thought the same, Child," he said. "But perhaps they were simply trying to do what they hoped was best, keeping themselves from really thinking about what they were doing. At that, they were far more merciful than some in our early history on the home world." He stared into the fire, his eyes gleaming. "And, of course, they wrote the beginning of this book you hold in your hands, though they had outlawed teaching anyone to read it.

"You will learn later that in the old days they made war in order to kill off excess population. Or they just pulled people out of their homes and killed them without reason, simply to thin the ranks of humankind. They had no qualms about it." He stirred the fire with the steel-shod base of his staff, but there were only scattered coals left, now.

Thom rose and said, "We must rest now. The yurt moves slowly, and winter comes behind very quickly indeed. We must be on the move with the first light."

CHAPTER THIRTEEN

The Dome

When the sun rose, very dim and chilly behind a thin layer of cloud, they were well on their way across the plain. The hooves of the boar-oxen kicked up puffs of dust, and the constant breeze tossed it into their eyes and up their noses. Hanne found herself sneezing, as much from the rapid cooling of the air as from the irritation of the grit.

She and Tomba kept shifting from side to side, front to back of the yurt, as the eddies caught up snatches of dust and flung them into their faces. The wind was coming in puffs, first from the south, then from the north. There was a feeling of uneasiness in the air that made them edgy and anxious to move more quickly. Tomba ran ahead, at last, to climb a hillock.

He stared ahead. Then he turned and waved to his family. "Granda! Hanne! There is a tremendous big yurt ahead of us. But bigger—or like a hill, but smaller. Come, oh come and see!"

When Hanne panted up beside him, she could see, at the edge where the sky met the plain, an undistinguishable lump that was surely no natural outcrop or growth on the soil of the plain. No amount of staring would bring it clear, and Granda had trouble seeing anything there at all.

Encouraged, they urged the animals onward, and every time they paused for rest they strained their gazes toward the shape, which seemed to draw no nearer. Night camp and their lessons barely distracted them from wondering what it might be.

It was three days before they came near that strange dwelling and saw it clearly. To Hanne's amazement (though she was not sure why, except that history should stay decently between book covers where it belonged), it was the very dome described in the history books.

"For the comfort and safety of the colonists, a large thermoplast dome was designed to be formed from naturally occurring silicates. Though not intended as a permanent base for any of the communities, it was designed to endure for generations as a storage area or a fortress, whichever might be most needed.

"However, the colonists on Heaven were deposited in a spot holding no fuel, little large vegetation, and practically no game. They were forced to scout farther and farther afield to find more hospitable country, for they desired to leave the emergency rations for some time of direst need. When one of the families found the hills beyond the northern horizon, they knew they could survive there, and they left the dome behind."

And there it sat, just as it was described. They plodded up to it beside the yurt, trying to soothe the alarmed boar-oxen, which had never seen anything like this huge dome thrusting into the sky.

The wind had scoured it with sand until the high gloss of its surface was dimmed, though spots still shone brightly. The arch of the doorway was empty, and they drove their beasts inside, Hanne tugging at their heads to keep them from balking. The calf, tethered to the tail of the vehicle, bellowed frantically, and the female kept trying to turn and see to him, but Thom flicked her back with the reins. It was a relief to get out of the wind, for it now blew strongly from the northwest and was growing colder.

Awed, the three stood in a vast bubble of space, peering upward at the curve of the roof looming high above them, filled with darkness. Every thud of Hanne's heart, every breath she drew seemed to echo round and round in that empty shell.

Outside, the clouds grew thicker as night came on, and it was getting darker and darker. Thom took his staff from the yurt and turned the collar that increased its power. Then, indeed, they were awed, for the inner surfaces of the place glimmered in a thousand refractions of green and rose and golden ochre. It was like being inside a rainbow, and Hanne felt her throat grow tight with a strange sensation.

Beside the entrance door, there stood a canister very like that in which the Holy Fire lived, though it was far larger. Into the metal casing was stamped,

LITHIUM REACTION MODULE
CONTROLLED FUSION

Thom read the words, examined the thing closely, and then twirled the top off and fumbled at its interior.

"Stand back," he told the children. "It has been generations since this was kindled, and I have no idea what may happen."

From the greatest distance he could manage, considering the length of his arm and his staff, he thrust the glowing tip of his bit of the Holy Fire into a tube protruding from the side of the canister. For a long while, he held it there, as Hanne held her breath and Tomba made little popping sounds in his throat.

After a time, there came a faint glow. That grew brighter, moment by moment, until blue-white light began flashing upward from the top of the thing, shooting far up into the depths of the dome. Sweating, Thom went close to adjust the control collar, bringing the energy-flow into a bearable level of brightness. Then he motioned for the children to go to the yurt.

"Unharness the animals, Hanne. Find their grain, Tomba. They have come far today, and they must eat and rest here in the shelter we have found. And while they take their ease, we may have a strange treat tonight. There was a stock of food left here, enough to feed the colony for months or years, in time of famine. If it is still good, we will save our own foodstuff and see if we like the fare our ancestors ate."

Hanne stared at him for a moment, before she went about her duties, thinking how strange it would be to eat food that had come past the very stars in their sky. Old food, older even than her grandfather.

When she returned to the yurt, she asked, "How did they make it last, Granda? Food that we store for the winter always molds in the next warm season, if we do not use it up."

"They had their own ways, lost now with much more. But I have read many times that their food would be good for centuries, not mere generations." Thom brought from a cupboard, whose door was an almost invisible part of the curving wall, three flat containers, whose silver colors reflected the brilliant light from the canister.

He set the shining squares into slots at the inner edge of the canister containing this new Holy Fire.

"But you can't cook on the Holy Fire!" Tomba cried. "It never gets hot."

The grandfather chuckled. "No, but the arts of our ancestors were clever. They devised a material that would be heated by the energies of this flame. This material allows the food to keep for many years, stored for any who might need it. I believe the food in these to be good, and it will be hot when I retrieve it. Believe me."

When they sat on the smooth, chilly floor of the old haven, their laps muffled with pads of blanket to keep their suppers from burning them, they opened the food trays with some wariness. A savory steam rose from the shapeless greenish mass inside. Unappetizing as the stuff looked, it was tasty and the food itself very filling.

When they were done, Hanne asked, "Will we stay here for the winter, Granda? There is food, and we have shelter."

He shook his head, the gray plait of his hair falling over his shoulder, as the blue ribbon of the healer braided into it gleamed in the cold light. "We would freeze, here.

"This place has its own system of heating. My father's father told me about it, when I was your age. But there must be many people here for it to work well enough to maintain itself. We three and our beasts make too little heat, for those systems use the body warmth of its dwellers, magnifying it to make the space comfortable for all.

"We will camp here for a time, using the shelter while we search out the lands to the south and west. There were reports written of small spots of sheltered land, with plants and trees.

"Not enough for the ten thousand of our kind who were here that first winter. Not enough even for the few thousands who were left at its end. They could only survive by going into the hills with the Greist."

Hanne thought of his words, as she made ready for bed. If they could not remain here, where it seemed safe, where could they go? The plain was bare and without food. What might lie to the south or the west that would help the family Thomas to survive?

* * * * * * *

A chilly gray morning woke Hanne. She lay for a time, listening to the morning grunts and groans of the boar-oxen and staring up into the dark vault above her. Ten thousand of her own people had sheltered here, all at once!

100

She was staggered by the thought, for she had never been in a group of more than twelve or so in all her life. The people had scattered over the wide expanse of the Gray Oak, and never had there been a reason for them to assemble, since she was born.

She blinked up at the tall curve of the doorway and the small shape of the yurt beside her bed-place. It seemed lost and insignificant in this cavernous space. The eerie feeling the thought gave her jerked her out of her blankets for her morning chores.

Thom smiled at her over the blaze he had kindled in the brazier they kept for use when the forest was too dry to risk open fire. They had a precious store of charcoal, burned by one of the families and bartered with the others for goods or services. The wood they had brought was all but gone, now, and the charcoal would not last forever.

"This morning," her grandfather said, "we will eat our own herb tea and cheese, toasted on oat bread. Though there is much of the Ship's food here, we are not used to it, and it may make us ill.

"Wake Tomba. We must eat and begin exploring for a place in which we can live. There is the promise of snow in the wind, this morning. We must find a warmer place, before the drifts come and it is too difficult to move the yurt."

When they left the shelter of the dome, Hanne could feel the keen edge of the wind even through the thickness of her shawls. The knitted Greist fur, which was shed once in every two years, was warm, but that blast from the north could penetrate almost any clothing her people could create.

Sped on by the nip in the air, they chose directions and split up to begin their searches. Thom went south. Tomba chose the west. Hanne angled between the two, into the southwest, with the wind at her back.

Though the plain lay in smooth swells and low hillocks to the north of the ancient shelter, on the southern side it broke into sharply cut gullies and rough hills. The terrain grew steeper and deeper and rougher as she moved, and she became nervous of missing something promising that lay in one of the deep valleys.

She kept to the higher ground, for that allowed her to see into the low spots on either hand. That meant, of course, she must climb or descend constantly. She scrambled up steep pitches of shale and made her way along ridges, which became higher and thinner, as the ravines and narrow valleys on either hand became deeper.

At midday, she stopped for bread and cheese and a sip from her water bottle. Unless they found a clean source of water soon, they would all suffer, she knew, and she kept her ears peeled for the sound of a stream, her eyes seeking for the glint of water in the depths below her.

Her legs grew weary and scratched, and her hands were sore with bruises and cuts from the stones. She knew she must turn soon, in order to find her way back before darkness began to fall. Yet a stubborn sense of urgency drove her onward, as the sun, hidden behind a rank of pewter-colored clouds, began to move down the west.

At last she saw, far to her right and between two worn lumps of stone, a speck of green. She was standing on the lip of a spur of rock, which seemed to have frozen like a wave as it curled toward the sky. She shaded her eyes, making a tunnel of her hands to bring the spot into sharper focus.

From the height to which she had managed to scramble, she could see, also, the glimmer of water, which was the same pewter shade as the reflected sky. Definitely, there was a fair-sized area of green there.

Hanne sighed with relief. She built a cairn of stones that could be seen from lower ground, and she formed an arrow of smaller rocks, pointing it toward her discovery. Tomorrow, it would be fairly easy to find this spot again.

She made haste toward the dome, at last. It was hidden behind miles of rough country, but she kept moving, despite her weary legs and her aching head.

Darkness fell long before Hanne was within eyeshot of the shelter. She had paused to build more cairns along her route, marking the way clearly for Tomba and her grandfather. If a Gurry-hound caught her before she reached her goal, still her family could find her discovery.

Before she was clear of the broken country, she saw the blue-white glare of Thom's firestick lighting the darkness, far away, toward the dome. She made a trumpet of her hands and gave the family call, "Arooeee!" Then she drove her tired limbs even faster over the uneven ground.

They met some thousand meters from the dome, and Hanne knew her grandfather had been searching for her. The thought made her sigh with relief. His smile creased his leathery face, as he stooped and lifted her as if she were still tiny.

"I located one tiny spring," he said. "I filled the flasks I carried. Tomba found a damp spot where many strange plants grow. But you found something more, I think, eh, Hanne?"

"It was far from me, but I could see water shining, even below such a gray sky. There were trees and grass, I am sure, for there was a lot of green." She lay back in his arms and sighed.

"It is a long distance, and very rough. It will not be easy to bring the beasts and the yurt there, Granda, if it is the place we need."

Thom bore her into the dome and let her down beside her brother. The boy had fallen asleep while he waited, and his grimy face still held a trace of worry.

"If that is the place we need," said Thom, "we will find a way to take our home there. Not lightly did our ancestors choose the yurt as the design best suited for the lives they were to lead.

"The wheels allow us to move when that is needed. The thick felts of the cover keep us dry and reasonably warm in winter, as well as sheltering us from the heat of the summer. There is space inside to allow us to live in some comfort.

"You have never seen the time when it was done, but this wagon can be taken apart and packed onto the backs of the boar-oxen. So even if we found an impassable spot on the top of a mountain or at the bottom of a ravine, we could still carry our yurt with us. The wheels are simply the easiest manner of moving it."

He bent and stirred a pot over the fire. The scent of dried vegetables mingled with the aroma of something delicious. "I added a container of meat-essence from the Ship stores," said Thom. "It flavored a stew that is better than good."

They ate in the flicker of the charcoal fire that mingled with the blaze of the canister. And when they slept, Hanne twitched and moaned, still straining to climb steeps and clamber down cliffs. She dreamed of water and of grass.

CHAPTER FOURTEEN

MOVING DAY

Deep in the night, the snow began to fall. The boar-oxen woke and snuffled and stamped their plate-like feet on the springy surface of the dome's floor, but Hanne didn't waken...not quite. She was weary to the bone, and her dreams had carried her far and deep.

Only the thin light of dawn brought her from her blankets to peer through the transparent ports in the great doors, which Thom had pulled together against the growing cold. The ground was covered with a thin layer of white, and the grasses around the dome were as stiff as an old man's whiskers.

"We must go today," said Thom, his tone grim. "This is the first light fall, the one we call the warning. When it comes, much more is close behind it. Hurry, Hanne. Make haste, Tomba. We must load quickly and go fast, or we will leave our frozen bodies in the snow for the Gurry-hounds to eat."

Never before had Hanne seen the yurt dismantled. Her very first memory was of the sacred omma symbol carven from wood, which swung from the matting of the yurt roof above her sleeping place.

She had lived all her life in the traveling tent, and she had helped to weave the Greist-fur matting and to felt the Greist-fur flaps, fitting it onto the hood-like framework. Yet she had never helped to dismantle the dwelling, reducing it to its components. It was surprising how little bulk and weight it made. One of the boar-oxen was able to carry the vehicle, the other being loaded with its contents.

With a travois-like arrangement to pull behind each of the family members, their necessities were possible to transport. What could not be moved at once they stored in the dome, for they could return when the weather permitted and bring the rest.

They took with them a large store of their own food, together with many containers of the Ship's concentrates. Blankets and shawls and tools were loaded onto the calf, which bawled dolefully, its tiny black eyes glowering at them from beneath its single wide horn. Even then, the pile remaining on the floor of the dome was larger than they liked, but they knew they must go at once.

"No one will come here, unless it may be another of the families, whose own Greist has come to its end. We will come back as soon as we can. Come, Children. We must go now," Thom said. He lifted his pack and stepped into the loop that went about his waist as he pulled his travois.

Hanne lifted her own burden and set the rope at her waist in the most comfortable position possible. She went out into the frosty morning, following her grandfather and

Tomba, whose complex tracks mingled with those of the animals.

The journey was not difficult, for some distance, and the beasts made good time, seeming to be glad to be out in the chill, clean air. They swung along on their padded hooves as if happy to be rid of the creaking and jouncing burden they usually pulled. The loads they carried were nothing to their heavily muscled bodies.

Soon, however, they reached the first gullies, and that began the hard work for both people and animals. Hanne led, taking the way she had gone before, keeping to the ridges so as to find her marks beneath the scanty snow. She called down directions to those below, so they could guide the beasts through the mazes of washes and rock-slides in the lower way.

Yet no animal could possibly have gone along those narrow spines of stone where Hanne moved, for the narrowing edges often crumbled and slithered, even under her own slight weight. Guided by her longer vision from above, Thom and Tomba were able to keep the boar-oxen moving in a fairly orderly fashion, avoiding time-consuming back-tracks from blocked routes.

Hanne found herself forging ahead of those below, however, for her markers guided her well and she went quickly, even with the burden of the travois. She found a stable spot on which to wait and perched on a stone to catch her breath, while the group among the stones beneath the cliffs struggled forward.

Her staff, a Holy Weapon she had never before been allowed to carry, was an encumbrance, filling one of her hands as she scrambled among the scree, trying to keep her travois straight and tracking behind her without overturning. Now it was heavy on her lap as she sat watching the last of the night's snow melt beneath the faint warmth of the sun.

She set its butt on the ground and let it lean against her thigh. The jingle of the boar-oxen's trappings came to her ears, mingled with the clatter of pots and tools. Those sounds, with the voices of her grandfather and her brother, told her just where they were, and she closed her eyes for a moment to rest them.

Her chin dipped to her chest. Her hand slid away from the haft of the weapon. The Taffte, which was traveling wrapped about her waist beneath her shawls, wriggled forth to curl in her lap, enjoying the sunlight.

Something tickled her foot. She moved it reflexively, but it couldn't travel far. The Taffte tensed and zipped from her lap as she came upright, reaching for the weapon. But the staff seemed to be rooted in the soil beside her trapped foot.

"Granda!" she screamed. "A creep-vine has caught me! Come quickly!"

Yet she knew in her heart no one could come in time to save her. The coils of the gray-tan creeper had come past her knees, now, covering the mouth of the weapon, though they shrank aside from the spark of the Holy Fire glimmering in its cup. She dared not put a hand to clear the mouth of the weapon, for that would only mean an even quicker death from the poisoned thorns of the vine.

She shouted again, in despair. The crunch of her grandfather's feet, the slither of his climb up the rocky slide to her position mocked her. The vine had almost reached her face. She inhaled deeply, as it covered mouth and nose, and waited for the first prick of the sleep-laden thorns.

Instead, she saw a bitter blue flare of light. There came a clenching of the vine about her body, with the smell of something vile burning. Then the creeper relaxed and fell away from her. She stared about, wondering how her grandfather had arrived so quickly. He was nowhere to be seen.

He came over the edge of the cliff at that moment, his eyes wide with wonder at what he had just seen.

"Hanne, the Taffte! That creature waited until the creep-vine was anchored to the soil by a single stem. Then it triggered the Holy Weapon by pressing on the stud with a tight coil. When the thing was burned clear of the staff, he pushed it to fall so as to sever the vine with the remnant of its flame. Who would think such a simple creature could think so well?"

He carefully removed the remains of the vine from Hanne and burned what was left with the fires of his own weapon. No bit remained to root again.

When he was satisfied she wasn't harmed, he put her staff into her hand and said, "Keep it tight in your grasp. When we are in our own place, we know where to look for enemies. Here they hide in different places. They adapt to their surroundings and change their color. Take care, Hanne!"

They camped for two nights on shelves of slanting stone, before they came to the place where Hanne had stood when she saw the oasis. When all three were on the high curl of rock, the sparkle of distant water was visible instantly, for on that day the sun shone brightly.

The cold of the past few days had not dulled that area of green trees and grass, and a haze of fog was just dissipating above the spot where the water glinted. Thom stared longingly at the distant vision, and Hanne caught Tomba's hand tightly in her own. Surely, in such a beautiful place, they could survive the winter!

They came down carefully off the height, joining the waiting beasts in the ravine below it. The way now was going to be slower, less certain, for Hanne had not yet covered the ground and marked a good route. The children would have to take turns exploring ahead along the ridges, while Thom led the boar-oxen and watched for predators.

In this country, there were probably Gurry-hounds as well as creep-vines. Those nasty creatures made their dens in broken country, under boulders or in crevices, and Hanne watched with some nervousness as her grandfather went ahead of the beasts, his weapon ready. She came behind the grumbling calf. Tomba was above, seeking out a passable route through the tumble.

They moved slowly, shoving from behind to make the boar-oxen move when there came a sharp drop or a crack in the floor of the gully. The sun moved up and over, and, when a Gurry came snarling and slashing from his den in a hole in the rock, the very habit of moving without mishap caused it to startle Hanne.

Thom was alert, and the weapon beamed its white energies to sear the predator, burning him almost in half. Yet the Gurry was driven by the ferocity that gave momentum to all its kind...it continued its course and crashed into her grandfather.

Thom went down beneath the weight of the pony-sized creature, with its fangs gripping his shoulder. His weapon was crushed uselessly against his chest by the Gurry's rib-cage.

Hanne leaped, only to have a round stone turn beneath her boot and send her tumbling. Tomba, above her, yelled wordlessly, and as she scrambled up he flung himself down the rotten stone of the ravine's wall.

Hanne, finding herself forced to climb around the spot where the female boar-ox stood bawling, her load blocking the passage, saw her brother slide down the sharp shale and the splintered layers to arrive, weapon ready. The Gurry was truly dead before it could injure their grandfather any further.

It required the combined strength of both children to lever the dead weight of the beast, inch by inch, off their grandfather's body. But Thom, old though he might be, was wiry and strong. He wriggled free on his own, when they had pried up the carcass of the Gurry, although he was gasping with pain from broken ribs.

"Wrap me tightly," he wheezed, when they had him flat on the ground, while the boar oxen stamped and snorted, alert and edgy at the nearness of the scorched body of the attacker.

Hanne rummaged in her pack after a length of bandage. Then she and her brother strapped the long strip around their grandfather, circling it about his ribs and pulling it tightly.

There came a rippling of gray along the length of Thom, and there was the Taffte. It flowed up the old man's body, waving its blunt and eyeless head as if to find its way. When it came to the injured chest, it wove itself back and forth over the bandage, as if to find the extent of the injuries. Then it wrapped itself around Thom, over the strapping, and tightened itself to hold the ribs in place.

Hanne stared at it. Then she shook her head, and Tomba and her grandfather echoed her motion. "What a strange creature," she sighed. "It seems to have no brain, but I am about to begin thinking that the entire length of it is brain. How else could it know what to do?"

"It is holding me, warming the hurt places. The pulse of its life comforts my pain," said Thom.

Hanne and Tomba took his hands and helped to pull him upright. Carefully, he stood and tested his legs, shifting his weight from side to side to see if they would hold him. Then he nodded with satisfaction.

"We will go on, now," he said. "I will stiffen, in time, and it will be much harder to move. Now is the time to cover as much distance as we can manage to. From where you were, Tomba, could you see how far it seems to the oasis?"

The boy settled a loosened strap holding supplies on the back of the male boar-ox. "Not far, now, Granda," he said. "We should be there before night, if nothing else happens, and if you can keep moving. It is beyond that ragged line of heights ahead, though we will have to turn sharply right soon, and follow the ridge around to the place where there seems to be a break in the hills."

The small caravan started out again. This time Hanne led, her hands clammy on the staff, her finger hovering near the stud that activated the Holy Fire. Thom came behind the beasts, using the calf as a sort of crutch, for he could rest his weight partially on the little animal's hind quarters, when he tired or needed support across rough places.

Tomba went high again, checking their route. Before they reached the end of the ravine they followed, he came pelting down again, his dark hair standing out from the flaps of his cap and his cheeks red with excitement.

"There is a channel just ahead. I think it may be where water drained away down into the stream ahead of us, back when there was enough rain to need such things. If we turn into it, it will cut off hours of walking. I could see almost to the point where it curves around the ridge and into the valley, Granda."

Thom looked thoughtful. "We will try it. I am not doing as well as I'd like, and my strength is going. This rough footing, even with the help of the calf, is draining me."

When the channel angled off from their route, they turned into it, beating the animals to make them enter the narrow track, which was almost covered at the top by the overhanging cliffs. Inside, it was cold, as if the blast of early winter that had brought the snow was still lingering there. Hanne thought it would probably be very cool even in the full stress of summer, when the sun burned this land harshly.

Thom still leaned on the calf, which did not appreciate the closeness of someone drenched in Gurry blood. But the space was so narrow the creature couldn't even buck, and they went forward without incident, slowly but without halting. When they rounded a sharp angle of stone, at last, and looked out into a space that held the gleam of water and the soft green of living plants, the sun was almost down.

They were, Hanne knew, now deep in the maze of the canyon lands she had seen from her high position. This was the deepest canyon she had seen, and it angled into their narrow cut, sloping down to a river that flowed, shallow and dark, between flat slopes of grass backed with trees and shrubs and, even more distantly, with the ochre-washed walls of stone in the sunset light.

The tangle of bushes and vines was very dark green, and the trees had silver bark and wide leaves whose upper surfaces reflected the orange light of the sun, now almost lost behind the cliffs. After the sameness of the gray-oak forest, the place was almost too colorful.

Over the valley hung a warm, damp haze. It didn't quite blur the outlines of the growing things, but it softened edges, so the place seemed like a vision in a dream...or like a mirage. At the right, where another cut slanted into the valley, there was a column of smoke—or of steam?

"Hot springs!" Thom said, holding himself against the pain of his ribs. "See the steam? Look... there in the dark cleft. There, I feel sure, we will find hot waters bubbling out of the rock. Hanne, bring the animals to the water. They have been on short rations for too long.

"Tomba, run ahead and pick a spot for our camp. We must settle in a bit, while I am still able to put the yurt together. It is too large a job for the pair of you, for your arms and legs are too short to stretch it."

There was no need to urge the boar-oxen toward the river. They raised their bristly heads, their tusks gleaming red in the light, and made for the water at a clumsy gallop. Their padded hooves made pluffing sounds on the moistening soil underfoot, and they ran right into the water. They stood, hock-deep, and began drawing in long, slurping draughts of the cold liquid, as Hanne and Tomba began unloading them.

The water was chill about her bared legs and feet, but Hanne untied and unbuckled ropes and straps, handing parcels of flaps and fabric and armloads of the gray-oak staves to her brother. Tomba deposited his loads on the bank in a heap, and when Hanne was finished with unburdening the animals, the two carried the materials to a sheltered space against the canyon wall, making trip after trip until all was safely deposited there.

The place Tomba had found was an excellent one, well shaded by a tremendous tree. Layers of dropped and drifted leaves made a soft carpet underfoot, and Hanne scuffed her toes in the aromatic layers, watching Thom set the staves in place on the frame of the yurt.

Her grandfather left off the wheels that had always underpinned the yurt. That told Hanne something very strange and important. Their wandering days might well be over...and if they were not, their travels, in this harsh countryside, must be afoot. The long routine of travel to summering and wintering grounds in the wheeled wagon was a thing of the past.

She helped the two stretch the cover onto the staves and to tie it down with the cords attached for the purpose. At last her home stood beneath the tree, a low gray hut, rounded and comfortable and rooted at last on the soil, no longer capable of travel on its own.

When all was secure, Hanne looked up at her grandfather. "If you feel like building a fire, Granda, Tomba and I will bring water from the river. You need to be washed, and the hot water may help your ribs to feel better," she said.

"If there was time before night, we might take you to that hot spring and let you soak away your pain. But for now, we will do what we can."

Thom nodded and squatted to build a pyramid of twigs and clicked together the special stones, which threw off sparks to make flame in tinder. The water was soon brought and the pot hung over the resulting fire.

It was not easy to help Granda out of his stiffened clothing. Hanne carried the long shirt and the loose breeches at arm's length toward the river, where she anchored them with rocks and allowed them to begin soaking clean. The stench of the Gurry's blood almost made her ill, as she walked away, but the smell was even worse on her grandfather's skin.

The Taffte wound itself off the old man and coiled around the base of a staff. Hanne thought it was watching them, as they helped Thom to cleanse himself. That took some time, for now he was stiffening, his bruised bones and muscles protesting every move.

When he was clean and dressed in fresh clothing, he leaned against the side of the yurt and sighed. "We have come to a good place, Hanne, Tomba. There is water that will never run dry, if it still is here at the end of the long dry season. There must be food among the many kinds of growing plants and in the river. We will survive in this fertile spot. I see it in my heart."

Hanne comforted herself with his words, when she lay inside the yurt once more, huddled against Tomba in the darkness.

CHAPTER FIFTEEN

The Magical Valley

She woke softly, quietly, feeling, for the first time in weeks, comfortable inside herself. From her warm nest of blankets, she could hear the murmur of water over worn rocks. The trill of a winter bird sounded from the tree above the yurt. A leaf whispered down the felt of the roof, and outside a last chorus of insects chirped goodbye to summer.

Nearer at hand, she could hear her grandfather's burring snores. They had punctuated her sleep for all of her life, and now the sound told her she was at home and everything was well.

She closed her eyes, and when she opened them again the light slanting through the door flap was bright. It was time to get up and explore this new world to which they had come.

They boiled a mush of oats for breakfast. Thom ate little, and Hanne could see he was in pain, though he said nothing about it. His eyelids were bluish, and there was a new and deeper crease between his brows. She knew she must find the way to the hot springs, so the warm water could restore her grandfather to something like ease.

"We will go and look for the spring," she said, when she had helped to settle him on his pad in the yurt.

He grunted and opened his eyes. "That is good. Go quickly, child, for I feel as if I had been trampled by all the boar-oxen in the Gray-Oak Hills."

Tomba yawned and stretched, and she wiped away the remnant of his mush that had circled his mouth. "We will go now," she said. "Perhaps there will be wild plants back there in the tangle that we can learn to cook and to eat. Where there is damp and good black soil like this, there should be mushrooms, too."

"Never eat one until I have tested it!" warned Thom, without opening his eyes.

Hanne sighed. "I've known that since I was a baby," she grumbled, as she put on her shawls against the brisk air of the morning.

Tomba followed her outside, and they stared for a moment at the thick line of shrubbery edging the small glade in which they had put the yurt. It looked dense and prickly, but that was the direction, and there they had to go.

It was just as hard to penetrate as it had looked. Hanne and Tomba struggled through thorny bushes and grasping vines, leaving behind bits of hair and skin and shawl as they went. But among the thorns grew small bright fruit, which gave off a winy scent that smelled delicious. Hanne gathered a handful and put them in her pouch.

The boar-oxen had a certain instinct for poisonous foods. If they ate these attractive morsels, it would be safe for her family to try them, as well.

She pushed forward, breaking a trail for Tomba, whose short legs made hard work of such matters. Beyond several layers of the thorny shrubs, they found a narrow path, whose steep sides were composed of worn-away branches. Some animal used this track, that was certain.

She bent to examine the soil for footprints, and there she saw the distinctive paw print of a Gurry. She shivered. Not even here, so far from all she knew, could they be safe from the dangerous beasts!

The track was old, bits of dirt having fallen from the sides and blurred its edges. She felt it was safe to use the path now—it would be night, probably, before the beast came again to the water.

There came a plopping sound, as they moved along, growing louder and louder as they neared the stone cliff. In a few more paces, the track veered, and Hanne could see a pool of boiling mud. Big brown bubbles swelled atop the thick pool, growing to huge size before they popped with sloppy smacks.

Beyond the pool, a narrow stream of steaming water welled out through a cleft in the rock of the ravine's wall. The water from that flowed down through grayish sand to the pool, and in the wet areas grew a multitude of plants. Some were, she noted with sudden joy, familiar herbs and wild vegetables she had known in the Gray Oak. They had grown, through the winters, beneath the warm cover of the Greist, staying fresh for those who lived in the warmth of the great creature.

There were, of course, many that were strange to her, but Hanne knew that the animals could test those out for her. They looked, some of them, very crisp and juicy, while others were leafy. With green stuff to add to their diet, they would remain healthy. Here in this sheltered place, warmed by the hot spring, winter would not, she felt certain, touch this wild garden.

Hanne felt Tomba leave her side to step forward and look down into the mud. "This will heal Granda's hurts," he said, almost to himself. "We must bring him here and plaster him with it, over and over. The heat and the damp will help, and there is something else, too. Do you smell that, Hanne? It smells like the salve Granda uses, sometimes."

She sniffed the sulfurous scent and nodded. Now their own healer needed a healer for himself, and it seemed they had found something that would help him.

She sighed with pleasure. This was a magical valley, supplied with many things that would make their lives easier. It was obvious why her people had ignored it, when they left the dome. There was not enough space here for more than a handful of people. The thousands who had left the dome before that second winter could never have fitted into the available space, much less survived here.

She looked about and nodded. Reaching into her pouch, she drew out a strand of the Greist's fur and tucked it into a cranny in the stone wall, weighting it with a pebble. She moved up the cleft for some distance and found another likely spot, where she planted more strands.

Tomba watched her with approval. "If I were a baby Greist, I would love it here," he said. "Our Greist used to tell stories about a place where it was warm in the winter and the plants never froze. Do you suppose this was the very spot?"

She shook her head. "I suspect there may be many places like this," she said. "Perhaps enough for all of the families to have one, if they search far and carefully enough.

"When all the old Greist are dead, and our own dear Greist told me the time has come for all his generation to die, our people will need something to warm them and keep them safe through the winter. It will be a long, long time before young Greist grow big enough to help us again."

She bent and caught up a handful of the rich black dirt. "I will plant bits of our Greist everywhere I can. One day there will be Greist here, and that will force the Gurries to move away. The Greist always kept them off, during the winter, and they should do the same here. Then it will be safer."

"Do you suppose we might get some of the other families to come here, next summer when it's warm enough to travel again?" asked Tomba, bending to examine a tuber he had unearthed with the toe of his skin shoe.

"We might form a whole new colony, down here in the south." Hanne sighed. Then she went back to the spot where she had left the pots in which she intended to carry hot water for Granda.

"We will have a good winter here, Tomba. We can play with the Taffte. We know how to make stories, because we learned from our old Greist. We will tell stories and study with Granda, and before we know it winter will be over. There is a great deal to do!'

She let the flowing water steam into the pots. Then, each carrying a double burden, the two turned back toward the yurt where grandfather waited.

Once again, the family Thomas was finding a new way for the people who lived on Heaven.

CHAPTER SIXTEEN

STRANGE SOUNDS AND SILENCES

It took some time, the next morning, to get Granda to the pool of hot water. He was hurt worse than Hanne had thought, and when he woke, stiff and sore, it was all he could do to hobble out to the bushes to relieve himself, and even then Tomba had to help him as if he were a baby.

Then the old man was exhausted. The broth Hanne boiled had to wait until he awoke; by then it was cold and had to be warmed all over again, and Hanne was so worried that her hands shook as she held the bowl for her grandfather.

"Do not worry," he said, spooning up the last of the soup. "I am not so old and frail that a Gurry can put me out of action. Let me rest a bit, and then we will see if I can make it to this famous hot pool of yours."

While he rested again, Hanne left Tomba to watch over him and began exploring the small plot of ground that comprised their tiny valley. The rock was steep, walling it in securely. Only the narrow pass along the stream and the other that let them through the ridge seemed to give access to it at all.

The western end, through which the river entered the valley, was a pinched-in neck of hard, green-black stone no more than a couple of arm-spans wide, holding in a swift, deep torrent of water. The ravine leading back into the cliffs from which the brook flowed seemed too narrow at its farther end to extend very far.

No person or animal could, she thought, fight its way upstream against the river's current, and only fishes and water animals could come down from that direction. If she could manage to fence off the other approaches, perhaps no

Gurry would be able to get in to attack their boar-oxen or themselves.

Of course, there was already one, at least, of the beasts in the ravine where the hot springs flowed, but she would worry about that when she could find the time. For now, she was planning strategy, and it was only when she turned back toward the yurt that she realized she had been doing exactly the sort of thing she had, all her life, seen her grandfather do.

By the time she had made a circuit of the grass-patch, skirting the overgrown edges near the cliffs and estimating their area and their makeup, she was hot and thirsty. Here in this cup of stone, the cold wind had not yet succeeded in chilling the air, and the steam from the springs laid a sort of lid over the valley. When she knelt beside a brook that wandered from a clump of blue-green bushes and ended at the river, she found even the water warmer than was agreeable.

She found Granda awake, when she returned to the yurt, and Tomba, in his turn, was stretched on his stomach, his cheek buried in the blanket, sound asleep. She shook him awake and turned to help her grandfather to his feet.

The Taffte came wriggling out of some fold of the bedding and wound its way up her leg, to wrap at last about her waist. For some reason, the dry, pulsing warmth of the creature was very comforting to her, and she was glad it was there, as she and her brother helped the old man toward the springs.

The air in the ravine was warm and humid. The ferns leaning from crevices in the walls and the thick-stalked plants growing in the black mud at the water's edge dripped with moisture. Hanne had never seen a country like this one, and she breathed deeply, relishing the strangely scented air.

There was the fragrance of flowers, as well as the tang of the fruit they had found earlier, even now at the edge of winter. What might they find, when there was time to explore this winding cut in the rock?

Then she turned her mind to helping her grandfather shed his robes, as he moved into the steamy liquid mud. Once he was sitting, the level came above his chest, and he pushed himself back against the rocks at the end of the slight hollow, while the two children plastered his ribs with hot black handfuls that smelled of sulfur and less identifiable things.

He had been pale, his face lined with marks of pain. Now Hanne saw a trace of color rising into his thin cheeks. The lines gradually smoothed away, as the warm mud was renewed, every time it cooled.

She stroked it on, as Tomba pushed up piles of the stuff, ready to her hand. By the time the third application had been used, the boy was as muddy as their grandfather, and she sent him farther upstream to wash himself in the hot water of the brook.

Granda let himself slide into the pool until only his chin was out of the hot muck. He looked, now, more like the person she had known all her life. His eyes were closed, and the dark lines had left his forehead. The heat and the steamy air were combining to soothe his injuries and to help them heal.

Tomba was splashing in the water, moving upstream and around a knee of stone. Hanne found herself nodding, her eyes closing in this sleepy atmosphere. She put her head onto her knees and closed her eyes.

A shriek woke her. She was on her feet before her mind had time to engage, her hand reaching for her staff, her eyes sweeping the area about the spring. But the cries came from upstream—where Tomba had gone!

She pushed through a thicket of spice-scented growth and found a small path along the bank. "Tomba!" she shouted, moving as fast as possible toward his frightened voice.

Then she was around the bend and could see what had terrified her brother. He was backed into a narrow cranny of rock, up to his neck in water. Facing him, across the width of the hot stream, was a Gurry, its wicked muzzle lowered, its stiff ears cocked toward its intended prey. It was gathering its skinny haunches under it for a leap when the blaze from her staff touched its back.

The beast turned, quicker than a thought, and bounded toward her. She backed a step, as the ugly snout raged toward her, the double row of teeth drooling saliva and the eyes blazing with furious hunger. Again, she energized the staff, blasting a bright tunnel through the fragrant air of the ravine. But she missed, and the Gurry was almost upon her.

Suddenly, Hanne realized the pressure of the Taffte was gone from her waist. Even as she shot another stream of the Holy Fire at the charging Gurry, the animal seemed to stumble, plowing forward onto its hairless nose.

She stepped forward and bored a hole through its skull with the focused energy of the staff. Then she looked about to find the reason for its uncharacteristic fall.

The Taffte was knotted deftly about its front forelegs.

"Tomba, come here," she said, over her shoulder, to her shivering brother. Her own voice was quivering, she found. "You are safe, now. The Taffte tripped the Gurry, and I finished it off. You can come out, now."

She could hear the sloshing of water as he waded toward her. She pictured in her mind his scurry toward the spot downstream where he had left his clothing. Boys! As if she hadn't changed his moss-padded diapers when he was tiny!

She stared down at the dead Gurry. In this atmosphere, it would decay quickly. She knew they would need to give her grandfather more treatments in the healing mud and water, until he was well over his injuries, and the stink of rotting flesh would be of no help to him.

Gurry meat was rank and made people ill. What could she do with the carcass, if she managed to move it at all? But the hide, now, was another matter.

Without a Greist to provide its sheddings for fiber, they were going to have to find new ways to make clothing and bedding and flaps for the yurt. That hide might be dirt-colored; the fur might be scanty and coarse, but it would be a handy bit of material, once she had it removed and cured.

Without thinking again about her frightened brother, Hanne narrowed the beam from her staff to a blade-like thinness and sliced the dead animal from neck to tail. Tomba might scoff at this unattractive addition to their supplies, but she suspected they would do stranger things than this, as they learned to live in this alien place.

It took a long time to skin out the Gurry, and Tomba returned to help, after he assisted Granda out of the pool. "He's sitting against the rock wall, sleeping, I think," the boy told her, as he tugged hard at the head of the beast, while she peeled the skin back, as if removing a coat, from the upper body and the forelegs. The stink of the rank blood and the mangy hide was sickening.

She wiped a bloody hand against a clump of ferns and used it to push her hair back from her face. She was hot, in this muggy place, but she did not intend to rest until the task was completed.

"He'll be warm and comfortable, while we get this done," she grunted, seizing the hide again, while Tomba shifted his grip to allow her to peel it from the hind quarters. The thin strands of flimsy tissue that bound the skin to the flesh stretched and tore, and the fur rolled back, baring the bony limbs and ribs.

The naked carcass was skinny and ugly, when they had removed the fur entirely. She reduced it to a pile of pale ash with the energies from her staff, while Tomba sorted the teeth they had knocked from the wicked mouth into handy sizes.

The bones, still steaming amid the ash, would possibly be useful, too, when they had dried and cured them. Splintered, they would make awls and needles. The larger ones would make stakes to tie down the yurt-tent.

They returned in triumph to the pool, to find Granda waking from his nap, his eyes clear and his body now able to move with more ease than before. "We will do well, here, Hanne," he said, eyeing the bloody hide. "You will find the skin will cure, if you put it out on the grass beside the yurt and scrub it with pebbles and then with sand and ash from our fires.

"There may be salt springs in this area, as there are in the Gray-Oak hills, and we can treat it with salt. We'll stretch it on frames made from the tree-switches along the stream, and when it is done it will make a warm cloak or a sleeping fur for one of us."

Tomba grimaced. "It's ugly," he said. "And it smells."

Thom looked down at his grandson. "Many things are ugly that are also useful," he said. "Make no judgments, young Tomba. We will use worse things than this, before we are done."

CHAPTER SEVENTEEN

Learning a New Way

Winter roared among the heights above the small valley, sending sifting snow into its depths from time to time. Often Hanne woke to find the yurt's covering powdered with white, but always the warm breath of the hot spring melted it away soon after daybreak.

The mornings were foggy, and sometimes, if the sun did not shine, the mist remained all day. Then the shapes of the trees were ghostly, their branches dripping with wet, and Hanne and Tomba moved about carefully, for they were still unfamiliar with all the pitfalls of their tiny homeplace.

However, they did not mind the fog. They thought often of the bitter cold that must now wrap the Gray-Oak Hills in its snowy arms, and this warm place seemed to be almost a paradise.

Thom regained his strength quickly, once he began to heal, and he, too, found much to like about their new home. He cleared away the thickest of the brush along the track to the hot pool, making it easy to see any beast that might hide along the track, and they bathed often in the warm mud and the mineral-rich waters.

In its own way, the soothing water took the place of the hypnotic voice of the Greist, keeping their spirits high and their bodies active. Hanne felt that in some strange way the Greist must have guided them here, and she found herself thinking often of the wisps of fur she had planted about the nooks and crannies of the valley.

The boar-oxen grazed the length of the grassy span, and always there was fresh grass for them, nourished by the rich black soil and the steamy warmth. Another calf joined the first, and a day came when Granda decided the time had come to slaughter the yearling for meat and hide and tendon.

Hanne felt her heart sink. "Must we, Granda?" she asked, her voice choked with tears. "We have raised him from a tiny calf. He is our friend!"

Thom took her onto his knee, tall as she now was, as they sat before the yurt. He smoothed her hair with his rough fingers. "Hanne, child, this is a tiny spot. There is grass, yes, but only a little, and the calf is growing big and eating as much as his father.

"The new calf is a female, and by the time she reaches her growth, we will have the time to find another valley that will sustain a herd of boar-oxen. If we are lucky, we will have many of them, to provide meat and milk, but for now we must make a wise decision.

"If we keep the calf, and because of that we lose his tiny sister, we will only have one female, still, and our herd will grow slowly. And if the mother should die instead, that would be a disaster, for the little heifer could not live without her milk. We would be left with only two males, useful only for their meat, with no future boar-oxen at all. Think about it, Hanne, Tomba. What is the wise thing to do?"

Hanne gulped. She heard Tomba, beside her, draw a sobbing breath. They locked their hands together, and she said, "It is best he die, Granda. I can see that. But it is hard." The tears almost escaped again.

"Many things are hard, my children. We must be strong enough to deal with them and go forward. That is the secret." Thom turned abruptly and took up his staff.

"The Holy Fire is merciful, and that is a comfort," he murmured, as he turned the swift beam to the calf's broad head.

The animal dropped at once, and he never twitched again. It was, indeed, merciful, if it went through the brain.

The skinning and butchering were bloody tasks. This time, Thom showed Hanne how to draw out the tendons for use as cordage and to save the horn and bone to boil for glue.

It was plain the Greist had saved her people from a great deal of labor, providing its useful fur for winding into thread and cord, keeping plants green and fresh beneath its warm layering, and making moving about to hunt for food unnecessary in the winter. Now the family Thomas must make their own way, and Hanne found her back aching and her hands bleeding, before the grim business was done.

At last, the meat was cut into manageable chunks for later slicing into thin strips to dry before the fire. The hide was stretched ready for scrubbing and scraping the next day, and the tendon was strung neatly for later attention. As she straightened her back and followed her menfolk toward the welcoming pool and a hot bath, Hanne sighed.

This new life was not as easy as she had hoped. Still, she was with her grandfather and Tomba, instead of wintering with strangers, and that was something to be grateful for.

They drew near the pool and peeled off their bloody clothing. Hanne slid into a small pool beyond a rock, while Thom and her brother plunged into the big one. As she scrubbed her skin, she relaxed, sinking back into the warm water. Then she came upright, sending water sloshing.

Something unknown, its voice wild and shrill, was howling on the heights above.

She rose and floundered to the pile of her clothing at the edge of the water. Even as she tied cords and fastened wooden buttons, she was thinking desperately: That was no Gurry. That shrill howl was nothing she had ever heard, and it sounded both hungry and very near.

She took up her staff and ran toward the pool where Thom and Tomba bathed. She found them also dressed, staring up toward the stony lip, a hundred yards above their heads. The single voice was joined by another—and another! There was a pack of animals up there.

She shuddered and hurried after the others, who were speeding toward their grassy valley. So many creatures, if they wanted meat, would not trouble themselves with people. They would want the big bodies of the boar-oxen, and that could not be allowed to happen.

The time had come to build their barriers, so nothing could get into the safe confines of their little cup of ground.

CHAPTER EIGHTEEN

A Winter Without a Greist

Winter set in, on the lands above and beyond the craggy hills. Scanty snow fell, at times, into the small valley, whitening the dried grass and making the boar-oxen throw up their heads and snort, becoming almost frisky in the brisk weather.

No predator had come into the valley to endanger them, as yet, much to the relief of Thom and his grandchildren. So far their barriers of brush and stone had kept intruders away.

Thom went almost every day to bathe in the hot spring, and the children made it a habit to go with him. The steam and the minerals in the water seemed to ward off illness. Or perhaps it was as Thom suggested—sickness is caught from other people, and here they had nobody but themselves. However it was, Hanne felt unusually strong and well, and her Granda improved from week to week.

Tomba was a constant pain to both of them. His energies found no real outlet, for they could not risk allowing him to explore the system of ravines and streams alone. Where there was one Gurry, there had to be more.

They still heard howls, high above on the ridges at night. Besides, there were probably dangers they could not guess, very different from those they knew in the hills beyond the flat country.

They missed their Greist. Never in their lives had any of them lived through a winter that was not enlivened by the tales the great rug-like creature spun into their minds, as they lay stroking its fur. Now they found the days too long, once they had dried the meat from the calf and stored it, along with the edible plants they scrounged from the valley and the ravine.

They had worked hard also to get a supply of wood that would warm them through the cold weather, though this proved more difficult than they, with their forest background, would have supposed. They had to watch the stream every day, catching any wood coming down from other valleys farther up. It was constant labor.

The Taffte was patient, in the evenings, as they stroked it and wound it about their bodies and their arms. But it knew no stories—or if it did, they were locked securely into whatever portion of the rope -like creature served as its mind. It warmed them, and it knew their moods, but it could do little to relieve the dullness of the gray days.

The ravine was, of course, always warm and misty. Ferns sprouted there, new fronds uncurling their fiddle-heads as the older ones browned and died, and Hanne learned those that were tender and good and made them into salads. Plants unlike any they knew thrust succulent sprouts through the heavy brown soil and bloomed, filling the wintry air with spicy scents. They found themselves spending much of their time there.

"Why should we burn the wood to warm our house, when we can be warm there?" Thom asked Hanne, and she found she agreed. She and Tomba hated scouring the river's edge daily to keep their supply from being consumed entirely.

As the three sat neck deep in the swirling water, Hanne felt something of the comfort the warmth of the Greist had given her, in those lost times in the Gray-Oak hills. Often, while the steam tickled her nose and her grandfather dozed, she thought of one or another of the stories the creature had dreamed into their minds on those long winter days when nothing but snow wrapped the hills.

"Tomba?" she murmured, swishing her legs about in the current. "You remember any of the Greist tales?"

"Mmmph!" He took his chin out of the water and shook his head. "Not really. They seemed to slip in and out of my mind, and once they were gone they never came back."

"I think I remember some. Maybe I could tell a story. And then Granda. And then perhaps you could recall one. We could amuse ourselves in the winter." She giggled, as the Taffte came wriggling past, his serpent-like undulations tickling her neck.

Her grandfather's eyes lighted, as if he had suddenly recalled some forgotten treasure. "You know, I do know a story, every word of it, which was handed down in the family.

"My aunt, who died when I was about six or seven, used to tell it to us, making us learn it and the others she knew, even though we would have preferred to listen to the Greist. She said these tales had been told in our family since the very first Thomases came to this world, and she called my favorite one The Elephant's Child."

Hanne sat up straight in the warm water. "Our own ancestors told this story? Where did it come from? Tell us about the story, and then tell us the story, Granda!"

Thom sank deeper into the water, his gaze turning inward, as it often did when he thought of the past. "My father's sister found and memorized all the tales every Thomas in the Gray-Oak Hills knew about our family.

"We came, our own group of Thomases, as a family: the mother was a widow, and she had five children of her own and another three who had belonged to her husband's sister. Van, her son, was our own ancestor, and he was the one who first found the Greist."

Tomba gulped a mouthful of water, sputtered, and said, "Van? What a funny name!"

"He had sisters, according to the tale, and one of them remembered stories her own father had read to her, back on old Terra. She told them to everyone and made all the children promise never to forget them and to pass them along to their own children, so they would never be lost. Her father had been arrested and taken away to die by the Overlords, simply because he loved stories and possessed books.

"The Overlords considered books dangerous, and they made them illegal. The very book from which you study our own history would be illegal, back on that old world.

"Our people wrote it themselves, on materials that were in the equipment supplies at the dome. Every generation, one of us takes up the task of telling what happened over the years when he or she has lived. And that is why it begins with the words of the Overlords, for the one who wrote it had heard them with his own ears."

"And they took her father away because of books?" Hanne found it very hard to grasp. There seemed nothing as harmless as a book. Indeed, among those who lived in the hills, books of recollections they had written for their own families were prized more than boar-oxen.

"They did. The book our kinswoman recalled best was one written by a man who had been dead for many centuries, even at the time when our people were taken away from their home world. It was a strange book, and her favorite story was the one I have named.

"She knew it, every word, and strange words they were, too. And I know it, and now I will teach it to you, as I did to your parents before you, and you will teach it to your own children. Listen!"

He splashed warm water over himself and stretched in the hot pool. His eyes grew dreamy, as he began, "In the high and far-off times, the Elephant, oh Best Beloved, had no trunk...."

"What's an elephant?" asked Tomba. "And what's a trunk?"

"I do not know," said his grandfather. "But it doesn't matter. The story is enough, without understanding it. So listen...," and he told the wonderful old story with just the right emphasis at just the right places, until both children were sitting upright, chin-deep in the water, their faces tense with listening.

His voice died away at last, leaving Hanne trying to visualize a crocodile—or an elephant, for that matter. Tomba was murmuring, "The great gray-green greasy Limpopo River, all set about with fever-trees."

"So let's call our river the Limpopo River. And these trees—they might as well be fever-trees as anything else. We can keep the story alive!" Hanne was delighted with her idea. "Are there any more tales, Granda?"

"Not word-for word stories, but ones she remembered the shape of. And I will tell them to you, but they wouldn't last all winter. Not at one a day or even one a week. Still, from time to time I will tell you one, and you will repeat it until you know it, and not one of them will ever be lost to our people; not as long as Thomases survive."

Hanne sighed, and she heard the sound echoed softly by her small brother. Tomba settled again to his soak in the pool, and she found herself wondering, for the hundredth time, when the Greist would hatch or sprout or whatever they did, from the tufts of fur she had planted in this ravine.

Yet the story her grandfather had told lingered in her mind. The "satiable curiosity" of the Elephant's Child reminded her very much of Tomba. She felt suddenly that a winter of entertaining themselves might not be as bad as she once thought it might be.

CHAPTER NINETEEN

A New Beginning

The winter passed, sometimes slowly, with dull patches that seemed unending, sometimes quickly, amid laughter and stories told by one or another of the family. The boar-ox baby grew, her parents became fat and lazy, and the valley remained safe and warm, a haven of peace amid the dangers of the Plain.

Once, indeed, the howlers came down to the fence Thom and his grandchildren built across the narrows of the ravine. Hanne woke in the night, huddled against Tomba beneath the covers, and heard sharp yelps and growls and howls. She woke Thom, and the three of them took up their staffs and trudged up the path to the spot where the beasts struggled to pass the obstacle.

They had built that fence of heavy stones and the biggest trees that came down the stream, tying them together with ropy vines from the heavy growth, as well as strips of Gurry-hide. It formed a lattice-work three times Hanne's height, which was just as well, for the creatures they found there were leapers of great agility.

As they brought their staffs of Holy Fire up the dark cleft, Hanne could see glittering eyes shining through the meshes of the fence. Red and green and gold they shone, and the chorus of angry howls grew louder. The cold blue light of the staffs seemed not to frighten the animals at all.

As they paused, watching the group of struggling bodies beyond the fence, Hanne realized some were trying to climb straight up, thrusting their hairy forelegs through the meshes, while others chewed at the thongs holding the fence together. These were not mere animals, like the Gurry-hounds. They could think, and they could plan. The thought made her shiver.

"I have no quarrel with you!" Thom shouted at the throng of beasts. "We do not threaten you. But I will not allow you to threaten those who are in my charge. Go!" He twisted the control ring, and the beam of blue fire shot out, a long blade of light that licked through the spaces of the fence and touched those who pressed against the barrier.

Three of the climbers fell back, their paws touched by the energy of the beam. The rest withdrew a little from the fence and stared through the meshes, as if studying this new enemy.

Hanne shivered, and she felt Tomba, beside her, quivering, too. Such intelligent assessment, coming from animals, was frightening. But Thom did not falter.

He shot a stronger beam through the fence, forcing the rabble farther up the ravine. Now howls of pain mixed with those of anger and hunger, as the pack retreated before the Holy Fire.

At last the group was out of sight around a bend in the cut. But still Thom stood guard, his staff glowing brilliantly, lighting the thick growth on the walls of the canyon to an unnatural color, shining on the ripples of the brook as they purled down toward the pool.

They watched all night, but when dawn lit the sky there was no sign of even a single one of the beasts that had attacked the barrier. They did not return, much to Hanne's relief.

Spring came as a change in the feel of the air. The wind no longer whistled over the ridges, sending gusts down into their valley. The sun became warmer, and the ice that had formed overnight at the edges of pools upstream in the Limpopo River was no longer forming.

The boar-oxen became restless. The bull lifted his head many times a day and bellowed his challenge to other boar-ox bulls, who were too far away to hear. The children became impatient with the restricted area in which they could move.

Even Thom, now recovered as much as he ever could from his encounter with the Gurry-hound, found himself persuaded the time had come to take the yurt onto the Plain, to put its wheels back into place, and to go again into the Gray-Oak Hills to find his kindred.

Hanne found herself strangely reluctant to leave the small valley, no matter how anxious she had been to go. They had learned many things there, in the days since they came. But they would return, winter after winter, she felt sure. Others would come with them, if the Greist did, indeed, begin to die, ending their long cycle of life and death and rebirth.

There must be other valleys, other warm springs, other green places where the families could live during the cold months. While the ten thousand who had come from old Terra could never have found space to live in the canyons and would not have known how to survive there if they had, the few hundreds now living in the hills could surely find refuge.

This was a scanty world, filled with dangers that kept its tenants fit and alert. It would never support the unthinkable billions the Book told about. The Gurry-hounds and the creep-vines, the predators and the cold winds would keep the numbers reasonable. She had never thought of those things as blessings before, but now she understood some things she had never thought about in her life.

She turned to follow Granda and the boar-oxen back up the way down which they had come so many months before. Tomba rode the bull, behind the load of supplies, swinging his heels against the beast's fat sides. The calf was big enough to carry supplies, too, and the cow bore the folded yurt.

They would find the Teacher and the other Healers. They would see old friends and kinsmen, exchanging news and tales of the doings of the winter. It would be good to see her own kind again, after this isolated time in the canyon lands.

She turned aside and ran to the mouth of the ravine, peering into the steamy depths. That was one of the spots where she had planted Greist fur. Was that something growing there, dark against the pale clay and the stone?

She moved into the shadowy place, staring at the tuft of dark fur that seemed to be growing from the rocky wall. She touched it with a tentative finger.

Warmth ran up into her hand. A tiny, almost indistinguishable sensation thrilled through her. This was—oh, indeed, this was—a new Greist!

She turned and ran after Thom, waving her arms and calling for him to stop. When she caught up with him, she tugged at his sleeve eagerly, and he looked down, waiting.

"Granda! Oh, Granda! There is a brand new Greist growing in the ravine! We will come back and see it, in the fall. We may not live long enough for it to grow up, but it is there, Granda! It is there!"

Thom smiled down at her. "I knew it would be. That is a place of richness and birth, that ravine. The little Greist will thrive there. And we will, indeed, return. But for now, Hanne, Tomba, let us go back to the Gray-Oak Hills, with our news and our stories and the long tale of our winter here."

Hanne fell in behind the calf, her staff in her hand, her heart singing with joy. She wondered if her ancestors, who arrived here in fear and anger, had ever dreamed that life could be so good.

This was a world that could be called Heaven, if you knew how to make the most of its modest gifts. You only had to learn how to live with it.

The boar-ox bellowed again. They moved into the tangle of canyons, headed once more for the forest where their people waited for the good news the Thomas family, once again, would bring to them.